THE MAN AND
SUITS STOOD A
ALLEY, CHECKI
TO

As if some ancient instinct in him recognized them, Mark held up his webbed hands in an invitation to friendship, demonstrating his bond with them.

A police car drove up, the voice from the loudspeaker ordering: "You two in the wetsuits. Just hold it where you are!"

Lioa and Xos saw the car bearing down on them. They turned, preparing to make a run for it.

"Wait, please!" Mark cried. "Wait. It's all right. We're friends!" But as he moved toward them, they joined hands and suddenly each reached out to grab him, sending an electric current through Mark which slammed him into a brick wall of unconsciousness.

As he fell to the ground in stunned helplessness, the pair turned quickly and fled toward the water. . . .

DEATH SCOUTS

MAN FROM ATLANTIS # 2

RICHARD WOODLEY

A DELL BOOK

Published by
Dell Publishing Co., Inc.
1 Dag Hammarskjold Plaza
New York, New York 10017

Dell ® TM 681510, Dell Publishing Co., Inc.

ISBN: 0-440-15369-7

Printed in the United States of America
First printing—November 1977

chapter 1

Two miles off Hastings Point, the Pacific was calm and sparkling under a high sun in a nearly cloudless sky. The old, white lighthouse perched on the bluff at Hastings Point stood out starkly against the blue sky, and shimmered a bit in the warm, rising air.

A soft breeze caused the outboard to sway gently, slightly more than the big, steadily rocking Chris-Craft a hundred yards away. A passenger on the fantail of the Chris-Craft lolled under a collapsible canvas awning which shaded her from the sun. The three in the outboard lacked such shade, but they were there for the water, not for sun or shade. Their scuba tanks were propped against the gunwales as they rested between brief dives into the pleasant, cool, clear water.

Dilly Brice, a slender, twenty-six-year-old fashion model, dressed like her companions in a black wetsuit, knelt in the bottom of the boat and reached out here and there to pick up bits of aluminum foil and paper refuse from their lunch. She stuffed it into a plastic bag and knotted the top, then jammed it under the seat. Leaning back against the gunwale, tilting her head up, and closing her eyes against the sun, she ran her hand through her long, damp, blond hair and sighed a pleasant sigh as the sun baked her already well-tanned face.

Her fiancé, Chazz Jameson, a twenty-eight-year-old architectural draftsman, lay back against the forward thwart, his lean legs resting on top of Dilly's. She looked over at his handsome face and smiled, but his gray eyes were closed.

Herb Wayman, a beefy plumbing contractor several years older than the couple, sat on the stern thwart and smoothed over a small tear in his wetsuit with his hand. He burped and looked toward the bow. "Hey Chazz, you finished with your lunch?"

"Who wants to know?" Chazz didn't open his eyes.

"You got a sandwich left there. You gonna eat it?"

Without opening his eyes, Chazz groped beside him to find the sandwich bag and languidly held it up toward Herb.

Herb stepped forward carefully in the bobbing boat and took the bag. "What kind is it?"

"Sea bass—what else?"

"I don't like sea bass. Next time bring salami."

"I don't like salami. You'll eat anything."

Dilly chuckled. She sighed again and stretched. "The sun's so great out here. I'd love to take his suit off and get an all-over tan."

"That's okay by me," Herb said, smiling as he unwrapped the sandwich.

"Forget it, Dilly." Chazz opened his eyes briefly. "His heart couldn't take it. I'm gonna grab me ten more Z's." He closed his eyes and folded his arms over his chest.

"You'd think he worked hard all week," Dilly said.

"Draftsmen don't work," Herb said. "They sit

around and draw pretty lines all day. Plumbing contractors—now that's work!"

"Why do you think I'm a draftsman?" Chazz said, keeping his eyes closed.

"If it's so easy," Herb said, "how come you're always tired?"

"Night work."

"Night work!" Dilly scrambled over to Chazz on all fours. "I do all the night work, you lazy bum!" She leaped on him and began to tickle his ribs.

He wriggled and laughed, and tickled her in return. She screeched and writhed. Eventually they both fell back, exhausted.

Herb took a bite of sandwich, grimaced, and spit it out over the side. He tossed the rest of the sandwich in the general direction of the garbage bag. "I can't stand all this romantic nonsense between you two any more'n I can stand sea bass. I'm going in." He rose, gripped the gunwale with one hand, and reached for his air tank with the other.

"You go in belching like you are," Chazz said, "and you'll blow up like a balloon."

"I'll let you worry about it." Herb buckled the straps on his tanks and blew into his regulator. "Least I'll be in the water. This sun'll make you crazy." He flapped his flippers against the planks and leaned over the side. "Hey, what do you think *that* is?"

"Hmm?"

"Chazz, look at this stuff in the water."

Chazz and Dilly rolled to the side and hoisted themselves up to look into the water.

A strange, dark, purplish stain was spreading over the surface near them. The stain seemed to be rising from beneath, spreading an almost oily sheen closer and closer to the boat. Their wondering faces were reflected in it, in wavering distortions.

"It's spooky," Dilly said. "What could it be?"

"Weird," Herb said, shaking his head.

"The Navy's probably trying out some new marking dyes," Chazz offered. "They're always messing up the water with something."

"Yeah, maybe," Herb said, unconvinced. "But if the Navy's doing it, where are they?"

The stain advanced to within reach, and Herb stuck his right hand into it. "Ow!" He yanked his hand back and looked at it. The dark stain had burned a diagonal slash on his skin. "What in blazes . . . ?" He held his hand out toward Dilly and Chazz, and they examined it.

"It actually burns?" Chazz asked.

"You're not kidding it burns! Like I stuck it in acid."

"Water's clear on the other side," Dilly said urgently. "You better try and rinse it off there."

Herb leaned over the other side of the boat and dipped his hand into the water. "Doesn't help."

"Let's get out of here," Chazz said, sliding to the stern and the motor. "Secure the gear, Dilly."

Chazz turned his attention to the motor. Dilly steadied herself against the side as she lowered the air tanks to the decking. Then she reached over the side to pull in the rope ladder.

Chazz pulled on the starter cord, but the motor failed to catch.

Suddenly, from the water where Dilly was drawing in the ladder, a pair of webbed hands emerged, stretched up above the gunwales, quickly grabbed Dilly's arms, and yanked her over the side and down under the surface before she even had a chance to cry out.

"Chazz! Chazz!" Herb stumbled across the boat to where Dilly had disappeared and peered, dumfounded, over the side. "What happened to her?"

"Hunh?" Chazz took another pull on the cord, then turned around. "Where's Dilly?"

"She's gone! Something pulled her over!" Herb leaned down toward the water.

The dark, webbed hands shot out of the water again and grabbed Herb's shoulders.

"Chazz! Help!" Herb was yanked over the side and pulled under, and his cries became gurgles.

"What the devil's going on!" Chazz lunged for the spot from which Herb had been taken. "What the—"

Another pair of webbed hands seized him by the hair and flipped him over the side, towing him quickly under the water and out of sight.

The outboard, now without passengers, bobbed gently in the waves.

The woman sunbathing on the fantail of the Chris-Craft stared at the outboard for a few moments. The last garbled cries reached her. She stood up. "Lou?"

"Yeah, honey." Lou came aft from the cabin. "What was that yelling?"

"Lou, those divers over there," she pointed a trembling finger, "something pulled them out of the boat. They were hollering for help!"

"Where are they?" He leaned over the stern and peered at the empty outboard.

"They're gone!" She put her hand over her mouth. "Something took them! They're not coming up!"

He spun around toward the cabin. "Get us over

there. We better take a look. I'm gonna call the Coast Guard."

He went inside to the radio. The woman moved to the controls and pushed the starter button, bringing the engine sputtering to life. She turned the boat and headed slowly for the outboard.

In moments, Lou returned and leaned over the side, gazing at the outboard.

"What'd they say, Lou?"

"Stand by, they'll be right here."

"Lou?" Her voice was hoarse and quivering. "What could it be?"

"I don't know. I hope you're sure about what you saw. I wouldn't want to be responsible for getting the patrol out here, and then have those divers just surface with happy smiles."

"I know what I saw, Lou! Something pulled them under!"

"Okay, okay. I'm not really doubting you. Easy as you go now, let her idle. We're about on top of it. You think I should get my scuba gear and go in?"

"You're not going in there! Not after what I saw!"

"No, you're right. Could be some kind of squid. Look at that strange slick. Like oil. Just on one side of their boat."

"What is it?"

She left the controls and they both stared down at the purple stain.

"Darned if I know. Maybe I should take a sample."

"Let's just wait for the Coast Guard," she pleaded.

He reached over and touched the surface of the stain and snapped his hand back in pain. "Yowp! Burns! Okay, we'll wait."

*   *   *

The old lighthouse at Hastings Point had been dim and untended for the last twenty years, having been replaced by a series of smaller, offshore, electronic beams that needed no light-keeper. But it had been built sturdily atop the bluff, and was strong enough to withstand the gales that blew in off the Pacific. Now, the tower stood just as it had for those many years, the prisms of the great oil-fed lamp reflecting the afternoon sun that beat down on the glass circumference.

The lighthouse rose from the center of an old Victorian house, which had once been the keeper's home. A widow's walk surrounded the base of the tower where it rose from the roof.

For years the house, too, had been empty, as had the several outbuildings spread over the bluff, which had stored the fog horn, the kegs of oil, maintenance equipment, and even firewood for heating the house in an emergency.

But now the house and other buildings were bustling with activity. Though the light never shone from the tower, the lights burned late in the restored old house. Over the main door was a modest but dignified sign, painted in scrollwork like the name on the stern of an old whaling ship: FOUNDATION FOR OCEANIC RESEARCH. Beneath that, in smaller, simple Gothic script, was another sign reading: MILLER SIMON, PH.D., DIRECTOR; ELIZABETH MERRILL, M.D., ASSOCIATE.

The Foundation was less than a year old. It had been the dream of the two young scientists whose names were on the sign. Or rather the two dreams, for each had arrived at it separately. A lucky accident had brought the two of them together just when newly heightened interest in oceanic research had prompted the government to invest in such a semi-private, imaginative, and comparatively small operation.

The two scientists had not known each other before the founding of the center, but they had known of each other's work. And they both sought the same thing: a facility with a high standard of excellence, on a scale small enough to allow the greatest flexibility in their common pursuits. Their interest was in the creatures of the sea, large and small, and to them the charm of their operation was that they were free to take their time, to think, to analyze, to explore, to discover.

The Foundation, or F.O.R. as it was called, had quickly developed to just the size they wanted. They employed twenty people, most of them researchers. The outbuildings had been converted into spare holding tanks, labs, and storage space for the files and equipment that overflowed the offices. Near the main house stood two huge antennae.

The house retained a quaint nautical flavor. The main lab was huge, extending from one end of the house to the other. The walls of this room were adorned with prints of great old sailing ships—whalers, racing schooners, packet ships that used to ply the Pacific waters. And alongside them were hung maps, old and new, showing sea routes, weather patterns, and undersea environments. Scattered about on walls and tables and benches and desks, in what would seem random manner to a visitor, were barometers, anemometers, scales, Bunsen burners, petri dishes, and dozens of aquarium tanks. Labeled with handwritten cards, the aquariums held colorful, mobile exhibitions of both plants and animals in dazzling, flowing colors. They contained nudibranch, abalone, sea anemones, sea cucumbers, octopi, decorator crabs —all manner of flora and fauna plucked from the ocean for examination, experimentation, and study.

Off the far end of this vast lab was the radio room, packed with round-the-world transmitters and receivers that could transmit and receive signals in all kinds of weather. In one corner of this jammed room stood a sophisticated computer bank, a solid and smug edifice which stored tons of intellectual data and made it available for quick recall by human beings whose own brains could not retain a fraction of this information.

Opposite the radio room was a spiral stairway leading to the upstairs bedrooms and baths.

The rear exit was on the sea side of the main lab; from it, a wooden stairway angled back and forth to the beach below. The front entrance was away from the sea. First one entered a hallway which led to several small offices, two of which belonged to the principals.

But Doctors Simon and Merrill worked mostly in the huge lab, and used desks tucked there between aquariums. Dr. Simon's desk was piled high with sloping mountains of papers and reports; Dr. Merrill's was neat with most of its surface clear. The two desks reflected not only different personalities, but different backgrounds as well. Dr. Simon came from academia, the ivied labs of several universities; Dr. Merrill came from the Navy, where she had achieved a high reputation as an associate in the Navy Undersea Center, twenty-five miles south along the coast.

But not all their work was done in the lab. Around the corner in the hallway was a set of sliding doors and an elevator which led to a tunnel to the sea, two hundred feet below. In the tunnel was the dock where they kept their strange, four-sphered, deep-diving research submarine.

On this day of the disappearance of the three Scuba divers two miles offshore, the two scientists were engaged in monitoring separate bits of research.

Dr. Simon, in a white smock, closely watched an aquarium in which a queer, many-legged fish stalked. It was a sea robin, a small beast that both walks and swims. The fish slithered over to a button installed in the side of the tank, and pushed it with a bony fin. A bell tinkled lightly. Dr. Simon smiled, took from his pocket a small bit of dried food, and dropped it in. The sea robin swallowed it instantly.

"See that, Elizabeth?"

Dr. Merrill stepped over to the tank, carrying her clipboard. Though both in their mid-thirties, in appearance they were as unalike as their desks. Elizabeth Merrill, a slender and neatly coiffed blonde with big blue eyes, wore a finely ironed white smock over a black turtleneck. Miller Simon's smock was rumpled, like his wild brown hair. He was short, stocky, built like a wrestler. Her white shoes were clean; his black ones were scuffed. They shared an intensely emotional nature, but while Merrill tended toward reserve and quiet thoughtfulness, Simon was ebullient, always upbeat, an outspoken, aggressive physicist.

Divorced, but holding no grudges or regrets, Miller Simon never felt defeated by life's problems, but welcomed them, invited them in, addressed them with keen interest. Solutions were poetry to him.

Elizabeth Merrill, never married but much sought after by several off-and-on suitors, was, like her cohort, quite willing to face problems, but she tended to be less lighthearted about them. She saw the problems in more personal terms, and worried more. In style, she was the more disciplined of the two.

However, both were dilligent, uncommonly so, and they shared an appreciation for discovery that drew them together in their work.

"Did you see that?" he repeated.

"I heard it, at least. He rang the bell and ate. Marvelous!"

"I knew he'd get the hang of it."

"What do you do if he wants food at night?"

"You mean if he rings while I'm asleep? Ha! He doesn't bother my beauty rest. I let him wait until morning. He's been a nocturnal feeder for millions of years, but I've been training him to eat in daylight. That's what this is all about."

"Poor fellow!"

"Not at all. He loves it." Miller leaned over the tank and wrinkled his nose. "He's healthier, and he's even gained weight. Got more color in his cheeks, more bounce in his step. It's better for him. Evidently, evolution goofed on him a little." He laughed lightly and turned to her. "Like it did on me."

"On you? Oh, Miller." She softened her voice, assuming he was alluding, as he occasionally did, to his unscientific unkemptness. "Why do you say that?"

"Oh, you know. My parents and relatives brought me up to take over the family ranch in Montana. . . ."

Like truly dedicated scientists, they were shy about themselves outside of their work. Their conversation was generally about impersonal matters, and even though they had been working closely together for months, they knew little about each other's personal lives.

". . . It was dry, rugged, and gigantic country. Awesome and, to some, entirely absorbing territory. But for some reason, somewhere along the line I began to find more beauty in tiny things—artifacts at first, like arrowheads in the soil. Then on a visit to the shore, I discovered the beauty of sea shells, which attracted me not only by their designs, but by the fact that they once housed small, living things. Then I took up with those fine fellows of the swamplands, the newts and frogs. Somehow the combination of those interests got me into deep water, so to speak. I was lured more and more to swamps, then lakes, and then the sea. The sea is endless and huge. But to me it is a reservoir of millions of small things. I guess I find bigger challenges in delicacy."

His words alone might have been ponderous, were it not for his light, almost giggly laugh.

"That's evidently why you got to be so good at it," she said, sincerely. "I mean, so good at *all* of it, everything from the sea, even those things a bit larger." They nodded to each other. "That's why I brought Mark here when we left the Navy. I told him we had to have the best."

"Kind of you, kind of you to say, Elizabeth." He patted her on the shoulder. "But of course we both know that you brought your own excellence with you. And while we're on the subject of mutual admiration, how're you doing on the salinity?"

"Okay, here's the scale." For all their banter, they never veered far from their work. She read the data from her clipboard. "With four-percent salinity we get a pulse of ninety. With three percent, ninety-six. With two percent, one hundred eight. And so on. As the salinity rises, on this side, we also get a pulse rise, but faster." She flipped over a couple of pages and showed him a graph she'd drawn from these statistics.

"Got it," he said, nodding. He turned to a small desktop computer and punched in the numbers as he scanned the graph. "Okay, that's in. Now we know how much, or how little, salt affects his pulse. What's next?"

"I want to correlate that to water temp." She turned and walked over to a large tank the size of an extra-long bathtub. Miller followed her. "Mark?" she called softly.

Lying underwater on the bottom of the tank was the reclining figure of a man, asleep and breathing normally. The name she had given him was Mark Harris. She had known him for more than a year, as long as any human being had known him. He had been discovered on a beach, washed up by a storm, unconscious and near death. Elizabeth Merrill had revived him and taken him to the Navy Undersea Center where, through long weeks of testing, examination, and monitoring, she had discovered him to be a creature of both sea and land, having in his chest not lungs but gill-like structures.

No one, not even Mark Harris himself, knew where he came from. She attributed his ignorance to some form of amnesia. When all the data about him had been fed into a computer, the machine had answered with a question: LAST . . . CITIZEN . . . OF . . . AT-LANTIS . . . ?

No one knew what the computer had in mind, referring to that mythological island of a supremely advanced culture which had supposedly sunk into the

Atlantic east of Gibraltar thousands of years ago. The printout triggered no recollection in Mark Harris. Where he came from, where he belonged, thus who he was, were questions he could not answer, no matter how hard he tried.

What became known about him, over the time of Elizabeth's tests, was that he could live in the water like a fish, never needing to emerge. But he could also breathe the free air, for a dozen hours or so, before it was necessary to return to water. In the water, he had enormous strength and agility, swam as fast as a porpoise, with an undulating motion, could dive to any depth, remain there for any length of time, and perform tasks that outdid the Navy's most sophisticated deep-water recovery machines.

On land he had strengths and abilities appropriate to a normal young man six feet, one inch tall and weighing 182 pounds. But in a few hours dehydration would begin, sapping him of strength and finally causing his breath to fade and his skin to blacken.

Except for the fact that his hands and feet were delicately webbed, and his eyes were an eerie, solid green, he looked quite like a normal human male. His body was lithe and well-muscled; his face had fine, strong features, his hair was dark and curled close to his head.

In the tank he was wearing the same unusual tight yellow swim trunks in which he was found on the beach. On the left leg of the trunks was an odd emblem for which he had no explanation—an image of a conch shell suspended over the tips of blue waves.

"Mark, can you hear me?" she asked a little louder.

He opened his eyes slowly, shook his head slightly to waken, and then nodded.

"We're going to change the temperature of the water now," she went on. "First, warmer."

Mark nodded and stretched languorously.

Dr. Merrill turned to a set of nearby dials. Just then a voice came over the P.A. system, the voice of Joe Foley, the radio operator.

"Dr. Merrill, I just picked up something I think you oughta hear. I have it on tape. It's pretty far out."

"Coming, Joe." She looked at Mark in the tank. "Be right back."

She and Miller headed for the radio room.

Joe Foley was a lean and wiry twenty-two-year-old with long dark hair whose prior job had been spinning records at a Los Angeles discotheque. But he was a supremely competent radio operator, and it was one of the finer satisfactions of F.O.R. that such a lad could be heard about through word-of-mouth and hired without having to prove his qualifications before some higher authority. He sat amid a jumble of electronic equipment. To either side of him was a typewriter and a hotplate, and in the small room behind him was a cot where he slept when he had to, or often when he didn't, just to be near the assemblage of expensive gear he took such pride in.

When Elizabeth and Miller entered, he nodded without speaking and immediately hit the button that activated one of his tape recorders.

First came the voice of Lou, the man on the Chris-Craft. "Mayday! Mayday! George Zero Four Young to Coast Guard! Over!"

That message was quickly repeated. Then, contrasting with his frantic pitch, came the stubbornly calm and professional reply. "This is Coast Guard Six-two. Go ahead, George Zero Four Young."

"You better get out here fast! Three people in a small outboard were just yanked over the side by something my wife says was weird-looking and they haven't surfaced yet! I mean it's really wild! Over!"

"Give us your position, George Zero Four Young."

"We're two miles offshore. I mean, two miles off the old Point Hastings Light. Bearing one-six-six. We're powerboat *Lady M*. We weren't any more'n a hundred meters from the thing! Over."

"Roger, George Zero Four Young, we read you. Stand by. We're on the way. E.T.A. your position about twenty-two minutes. You copy?"

"Yes sir! Hurry!"

"Roger. On our way. Over and out."

"And there's a stain in the water that burns!"

"Say again?"

"A stain! Some funny purple stuff in the water, burned my hand!"

"Roger. Don't endanger yourself. We'll pick up some samples. Coast Guard out."

"Hurry! The stain is disappearing fast!"

Joe clicked off the machine. "That's the important part. It gets crazier. He keeps calling. In later transmissions the guy begins to convince himself it was a sea monster." Joe looked up at them and smiled. It was not that he took such transmissions lightly, but it was his manner to smile when he delivered a communication he had been clever enough to record. It was a modest sign of satisfaction in doing his job well.

Elizabeth swapped a hard glance with Miller. They nodded to Joe and went back to the lab.

Elizabeth rapped lightly on the glass of Mark's tank, and he sat up, pushing his head out of the water.

"Mark, do you know of any purple stain in the water that can burn you?"

Mark looked at her quizzically, and didn't answer at first. Then he shook his head. "No."

Miller took a step forward. "Nothing, Mark? Nothing at all?"

Mark looked at him thoughtfully. "Many things in the sea can burn. Even your own kerosene can irritate the skin. But what you say—no, I know of nothing like that."

Elizabeth pursed her lips. "Mark, how'd you like to take a break?"

He smiled. "I was taking a break."

"Joe?" She raised her voice and looked up at the intercom speaker. "Call the Coast Guard and tell them we're coming."

"They just called to ask for you!" Joe announced back.

chapter 2

Elizabeth was at the helm of the speedboat, *FOR—US* (Foundation for Oceanic Research—United States), the wind blowing her blond hair around her ears and billowing out her thin blue nylon windbreaker. Mark sat in the stern, wearing his swim trunks and a similar windbreaker. Compressed-air scuba tanks lay beside him.

She guided the boat through the near-shore surf and into more gentle swells, aiming for the rendezvous spot with the Coast Guard cutter two miles off.

Powered by twin Volvo inboards, *FOR—US* made short work of the trip, arriving at the scene in a few minutes. Elizabeth throttled down as they approached the cutter. She could see the bobbing, empty outboard, and near it the larger Chris-Craft cruiser.

Deckhands on the cutter waved to her, and an officer picked up a loudhailer and called out, "Hello, *FOR—US*, did you monitor this, Dr. Merrill?"

"We sure did," Elizabeth yelled back through cupped hands.

"Story's pretty much like you heard it. You got any ideas?"

"Not yet. Just thought we'd take a look."

The officer lowered the loudhailer to exchange a

few words with another guardsman, then raised it again. "Okay, go ahead and look around. But watch out for any purple slicks. Stuff burns, sure enough. I have collected water samples for you." The crewman next to him held up several small bottles that dangled from strings around his fingers.

"Thanks!" she called, waving.

Mark, meanwhile, had been strapping on the scuba tanks, and now appeared beside Elizabeth with the tanks on his back and his face mask in place.

The officer looked him over. "Who's your new diver?"

"Mark Harris," she shouted, patting Mark on the back, "from Atlantis."

The officer leaned his head back in obvious laughter to make plain his appreciation for the joke.

Though there were a few Navy officers at the Undersea Center and in Washington who were acquainted with Mark and his capabilities, almost no one else outside of the F.O.R. staff knew about him. Elizabeth's deal with the Navy was that Mark would be available to help in certain situations, but that his true nature should be kept a secret for as long as possible. In that way she hoped to protect him from either harm or exploitation. She generally avoided telling outright lies—for falsehoods made her quite uncomfortable—but she did allow herself to deflect questions about Mark, and to engage in small charades such as the current one of having Mark don Scuba gear when others were around to see him dive.

Mark stepped up to the rail and dropped backward over it into the water, holding his regulator tight in his mouth with one hand as he had seen other divers do. Then he came quickly up under the stern of the speedboat, where a special hook dangled under the water. He slid out of his airpack and hung the tanks on the hook.

This done, he flipped over and dove straight down, his hands at his sides, his legs together, undulating like an eel.

The water quickly became darker as he went deeper. He soon reached the reef and passed its coral outcroppings. He continued down further until there rose to either side of him the mountainlike walls of a trench. He veered to the right to approach the walls, dipping lower as he went. He glided along the walls, surveying them closely while still angling downward.

Suddenly he stopped, backtracked a few yards, and edged up against the wall, feeling the rock with his hands.

A slash mark, like a burn, marred the wall there. He felt along the markings with his hands, and studied them closely with his eyes.

Then he backed off a few yards, looked up and down along the slash mark, and abruptly turned and headed back for the boat.

While he was gone, Elizabeth had moved in close to the Coast Guard cutter and accepted the vials of water samples lowered to her in a net. She stowed them in a sponge-rubber-lined case, which she had just closed when she heard Mark under the boat.

Mark took the scuba tanks from the hook, wrestled into the straps, pulled on the face mask, and stuck the regulator into his mouth. Then he surfaced beside the boat and climbed quickly up the diver's ladder.

Elizabeth watched him mount the ladder, and as he removed his face mask she saw that he was troubled. "What is it, Mark?"

He shook his head. "It's very strange."

The officer from the cutter called over. "You pick up anything?"

"No!" Mark whispered urgently. "Say no, Elizabeth!"

She looked at him, puzzled. Then she turned to the cutter. "We'll get back to you!"

"Right!" The officer waved and walked away across the deck.

"Mark, what is it?" She moved close to him as he sloughed off his airpack. "What's the matter?"

"I don't know. What I have seen is strange. I will describe it to you as we head home."

She slid behind the controls, talking to him over her shoulder. "But why did you want me to tell the Coast Guard you found nothing?"

"I am not sure. It just gave me a strange feeling."

She fired up the engines, and the exhausts sputtered and gurgled behind them. She slowly pushed the throttles forward, and the engines gave out their throaty rumble as the speedboat planed smoothly back toward Hastings Point. "You don't often have, as you call them, 'strange feelings,' Mark."

"No."

Ginny Mendoza, the Foundation secretary, was bright and bubbly and twenty-five, a charming woman with wide brown eyes, tightly curled brown hair, a pug nose, a wide mouth, and a small waist. She adored her job. Daughter of a Navy pilot who had been killed in action in Southeast Asia, she hated violence as she loved the sea. The atmosphere of the lab was perfect for her. She doted on the peaceful friendliness of the place. It was typified, in her mind, by the way Dr. Simon encouraged children to drop by either to look at things or to bring their proud discoveries for the good physicist's analysis and explanation.

And so she was pleased when, upon answering the doorbell, she saw before her two small breathless boys, in smudged short-sleeved shirts and dungarees and worn canvas sneakers. One boy, with tousled hair, stood in front of the other, his hands behind his back.

Ginny smiled at them. "Hi, there."

"Hello," the first boy said. "My name is Kenny Washburn. I'm nine years old. This is my friend Billy. He's eight. He's with me. I brought this for the scientist." He quickly held forth a biscuit tin whose lid was clamped firmly in place by a rubber band.

"Cookies? How nice. Come right in."

"No, not cookies." He stepped through the door, followed closely by his partner. "It's a thing I found. It's the strangest thing I ever saw. We ran all the way over." He took several deep breaths. Billy did likewise, keeping his eyes on Kenny. "It's super!" he blurted.

"Well, that's terrific! Want to show me?"

"I'd rather show it to the scientist."

"Okay. Wait here a sec, I'll see if Dr. Simon can talk to you."

"It's weird!" he said, his eyes widening.

"Okay." She held up one finger, then left to find Dr. Simon.

He was in one of the small offices poring over some papers in a loose-leaf file.

She rapped lightly on the jamb and stepped in. "Miller?"

"Hi, Ginny. What's up?"

"There's a kid in the lobby with something in a can

he wants to show you. He's *very* excited. I don't know what it is. He didn't want to show it to me. Should I have him leave it, or—"

"Ginny," he smiled, "I make it a policy to see all kids, at all times, whether they're very excited or one-hundred-percent bored and boring. Although, I must say, kids that are excited can never be boring. Enthusiasm is the most attractive of all human traits. Too bad it seems to diminish as we grow up. Bring him in!"

A moment later she brought in the two boys. "This is Kenny Washburn and his friend Billy." She smiled at them and tapped both their shoulders.

Kenny stepped forward, holding the tin behind his back. "Are you the scientist?"

"Well now," he swiveled around and put his hands on his knees, "I'm one of them. What have you got there?"

Kenny's face lit up and he swung the tin in front of him. "This plant! It looks like a big carrot! It makes purple ink! It was there in the water at Sunset Beach. It's really neat! You gotta see it!"

"I'm more than happy to. You want to open the can for me?"

Kenny looked down at it. "Do I get a reward?"

Miller chuckled and turned to pull open a drawer. From a stack of documents he took a rectangular certificate that said across the top: OFFICIAL DISCOVERER OF WONDROUS THINGS. A red, white, and blue seal was affixed to one corner. He filled in Kenny's name above the appropriate line, and signed it. "Here you go." He held it up. "This makes you one of us."

Kenny's mouth made a silent, grateful O. He balanced the tin on one hand and took the certificate gingerly with the other. "Gee, thanks. Boy! Wait'll you see this plant!"

Miller leaned over to look around Kenny at Billy. "Did you help him find it?"

Billy shook his head.

"Okay. When you bring me something, you'll get a certificate too. Now then. Let's have a look."

Kenny slid the rubber band off and snapped the lid. He blinked and his mouth fell open. "Hey! What happened to my plant? There's a stone in here!" He spun toward Billy, angrily. "Did you play a trick on me and take my plant out?"

Billy shook his head quickly, looking scared.

"Well, well," Miller said, smiling, "so at least we have a stone."

"It was a plant!" Kenny sputtered. "It made purple stuff! It's the truth! Somebody took it! It was like a big carrot!"

"Well, why don't you leave this here with me and go back and see if you can find another one. I'd sure like to have a plant like that."

Kenny wrinkled up his nose and cocked his head. "You want the *stone*?" He was saved from deeper disappointment by the curious fact that somehow the stone itself was worthy.

"Sure, why not? No stone is like any other stone. And as a matter of fact, this particular stone has some unusual characteristics."

"Really?" Kenny took the stone out of the tin and handed it to Dr. Simon. "But I really did have a plant like I said," he added somberly.

Miller smiled at him, tapped his arm, and said good-bye. The boys hurried out.

"Ah me," he said to himself with an exaggerated

sigh, turning the angular stone over in his hands. "The marvels of the unfettered mind. The problem with a plant that looks like a big carrot is that it most likely *is* a big carrot. Much as this, as poor Kenny pointed out, is a stone, just like it looks."

"Miller? Miller?" Elizabeth burst through the front door and strode through the hallway.

"In here, my dear. What's up?"

She came through his door, plopped down her case of water samples, and perched her hip on the corner of his desk. "Miller, I have water samples in the case. Mark dove under the stain. He says he saw a giant slash mark along the rim of the B Sierra Trench. It looks like a burn. And it wasn't there three days ago when he did that two-thousand-meter check."

"A burn?" he said rather absently. He had taken out a small pocket knife and was scraping the edge of the stone. It was habitual with him; as some people read all their mail, including the junk, for no other reason than because it arrived at their address, so did Dr. Simon take a sample from every mundane bit of sediment that crossed his desk. He put a tiny scraping from the stone under the electronic microscope and then dropped the stone into an adjacent aquarium. He put his eye to the glass. "What kind of burn?" he asked, peering through the tube at the scraping.

Elizabeth looked at Mark.

"From the reef downward," Mark said. "Perhaps three hundred meters. At a sharp angle. The marring was perhaps three feet in width, quite consistent."

"Meteorite?"

"It is my belief that a meteorite would not be so hot, by the time it dropped into the ocean, as to leave such a burn in granite."

"Of course not, no, you're right. What then do you suppose?"

"I do not know."

"Maybe it was—hey! I don't believe this!" He pressed his eye to the glass and beckoned to Elizabeth. "Strange indeed! Here," he moved his head away, "take a look."

Elizabeth bent down to peer into the microscope.

"Have you ever seen rock crystals like that in your life?" he asked incredulously. "They're like cells! Oval!"

"Where did they come from?" Elizabeth asked, still staring into the microscope.

"From that stone I was scraping."

"Look!" Mark pointed to the aquarium where Miller had dropped the stone into the water.

They all looked at the stone. But it was no longer a stone. It was a plant, or like a plant—indeed, some-thing like a carrot in shape, though gray rather than orange, with a smooth skin. And it was swaying, pul-sating, like a breathing animal.

"Kenny's carrot," Miller said softly.

"What?"

"The boy who brought the stone to me, Elizabeth, he said it was not a stone when he found it in the water at Sunset Beach. He said it was a plant, like a carrot. This same plant we now have here, I daresay. Come over here." He led Elizabeth and Mark over to a wall map and pointed to a shore area with his fin-ger. "The kid picked this thing up right here, Sunset Beach. See here?"

"Yes," Mark said.

Elizabeth nodded.

"He said it gave off purple ink in the water. And

this so-called burn was where, Mark? Here?" He moved his finger seaward, to the southwest.

Mark stepped up and planted his finger half an inch further west. "Here."

"All right." Miller put his index finger on that spot, and, using his thumb like a compass, swung it around to put it on the site of the beach. "And this time of year the tide and drift go like this . . ." He moved his finger from the burnsite toward the beach. "Hmm."

Abruptly he turned from the map, brushed between Elizabeth and Mark, and picked up the phone on his desk.

"Who are you calling?"

"I'm embarrassed to say." He put a hand over the mouthpiece. "You're going to think I've flipped." Then someone answered. "Sam Woodward, please." He stared at the ceiling while he waited. "Sam? Miller Simon . . . Fine, fine. Listen, by any chance have you people up there had any sightings in the past few days? . . . Oh really? Where abouts? . . . Is that so? . . . No, no, no special reason. Just checking on something. You know us. We're liable to ask questions about anything under the sun, even if we haven't got a reason. Thanks, Sam."

He hung up.

"That was the Meteorological Bureau?" Mark asked. Miller nodded.

"They saw something?"

"Day before yesterday," Miller said quietly. "Four in the morning, an orange and blue streak flashed downward and seemed to disappear into the sea fifty kilometers southwest of here."

"B Sierra Trench?"

"Yes, Mark. Right about there."

The three looked at each other.

"I think we should go out and have a look," Miller said. "Don't you?"

Immediately they headed for the elevator.

The elevator soundlessly took them two hundred feet down into the rock. They emerged and walked quickly along the tunnel and through the doorway into the submarine pen.

At the base of the cliff under the F.O.R. building was an old wooden boathouse. Behind it, dug out of the rock, was an opening from the boathouse into the sub pen itself. A deep channel connected the sea with the sub pen.

The conning tower of the nuclear-powered quadrispheric sub rose from the water. The small crew had already been alerted and was beginning to board through the hatch. In appearance, they were like the crewmen on a Jacques Cousteau excursion—dressed in striped jerseys, shorts, deck sneakers—but their casualness ended there. They were serious and strong and lithe young men, tanned and muscled, every one of them with extensive scuba experience as well as shipboard knowledge and skills. The crew nodded to the three visitors from the lab as they boarded.

They climbed down through the conning tower and entered the forward sphere, the control pod. The navigator and pilot were already in their raised swivel seats, checking over the dials. Elizabeth nodded to them.

"Okay, Wes," she said to the captain, a tall, broadshouldered man with curly blond hair, "let's go."

"Hi, Dr. Merrill, Dr. Simon, Mark. Welcome aboard." He turned to a control panel and pushed a button. "The con is closed. The con is locked." He scanned the dials and lights. "Let's take her out." He pushed another button, and a Klaxon horn rasped through the ship. "Bearing, Doctor?"

"Out of the channel, one-eight-five," Elizabeth said.

Wes nodded and turned to the second officer. "Set ten meters. Course three-four-three. Then one-eight-five at one hundred meters."

"Aye, Captain." The second officer punched the data up on his computer board.

The propellers spun and the motors began to hum. Water churned and bubbled in the pen. The con sank until it disappeared under the surface. The sub backed slowly between the pilings toward the open sea. Once clear of the pen, it turned a tight 180 degrees and pushed into the ocean, submerging slowly to one hundred meters.

Except to those on board, who were by now used to its design, even fond of it, the submersible was the queerest of undersea vehicles. Four huge spheres were aligned in a row from fore to aft and linked by passageways under a narrow steel deck. The conning tower was relatively common in configuration, perpendicular in front, sloping down in the rear, and perched on the deck between the first and second spheres. Each sphere had a ring of portholes. Remote-control cameras and sensing devices which could be focused in any direction protruded here and there. The front, control-pod sphere, had powerful headlights. The other spheres, which had less brilliant but still strong floodlights with which to illuminate the surrounding sea, were largely devoted to laboratories, computers, and research and communications gear. And of course there were the standard necessary fixtures, such as the galley and the sick bay.

The second sphere housed the airlock through which divers could enter and leave the sea. Near it was the decompression chamber where divers returning from deep and lengthy dives—except for Mark, of course—spent the required time under gradually diminishing compression until their bodies had readjusted to normal atmospheric pressure. A second emergency airlock and smaller decompression chamber were in the aft sphere.

The submersible's special construction allowed it to dive to any depth—even to the very deepest part of the ocean. Nuclear power permitted lengthy excursions. Not designed primarily for speed, the sub could cruise underwater comfortably at ten knots, rise and descend almost perpendicularly, and execute turns of a radius equal to its own length.

The black exterior of the submersible gave it a sinister appearance as it cruised through the depths. Its origins were, in fact, sinister. The sub had been the product of a brilliant but mad scientist who had attempted to develop an undersea habitat from which he planned a doomed maneuver to take over the world. Mark, diving for the Navy on an attempt to recover a sunken research submarine, had discovered the submersible, caused the habitat to be blown to smithereens, and followed this strange sub back to the surface.

Dr. Merrill was permitted to take the ship with her when she left the Navy to join the Foundation for Oceanic Research. She and Dr. Simon had stripped its innards bare, then re-outfitted it with the scientific gear with which it now plumbed the ocean depths.

Wes paced slowly back and forth behind his officers at the controls, overseeing every aspect of the submersible's performance.

"Steady at one hundred meters," the second officer barked out, "course one-eight-five."

Wes nodded.

Elizabeth, Miller, and Mark retreated to the second sphere, where they quickly checked over the diving and support systems, then they proceeded to the third sphere. There, surrounded by scientific equipment, they watched the course of the ship on television monitors.

The sub proceeded smoothly through the sea, its quiet, powerful engines barely audible. Schools of fish and squid and bunches of algae and plankton flashed by outside the port, illuminated by the exterior floods. Where the plankton was thick, the water took on a yellowish or bluish hue, like tinted fog. Startled squid left trails of black ink. Schools of big fish chased schools of smaller ones. Aside from the flitting animal activity, the sea beneath the surface was, as usual, serene. Where shoals rose under the craft, outcroppings of rock and coral glistened under the lights, the seaweed and sponges waving as if stirred by a sunny breeze.

Such seldom-seen views of the undersea world would captivate and charm ordinary observers. But to the two scientists and Mark, these vistas were not new. Although they stared into the television monitors or occasionally visited the ports to watch as closely as any enthralled landlubber, it was not to gaze upon the standard and commendable beauty, but to watch for signs of less common occurrences, signs of an extraordinary event, a visit by something which might have left a trail.

In time the sub entered the first section of the sloping chasm itself, the B Sierra Trench. The ageless rock rent eons ago by some unknown, ancient convulsion on the ocean floor, the canyon walls rose gradually higher on both sides. This undersea valley, like many of the ocean's submerged mountain ranges, rifts, chasms, and faults, was as dramatic and rugged as anything on land, the Grand Canyon included. The sea contained taller peaks and deeper troughs than any surface land could claim.

But they were not planning to go deep on this particular trip. What Mark had seen lay not far from the serrated rim of the trench.

"Wes," Elizabeth said into the intercom, "take her down to three hundred."

"Aye-aye, Doctor. Going to three hundred."

They felt the sub tilt slightly as the captain dropped her from one hundred to three hundred meters.

"Let's check all the video equipment," Elizabeth said, "all the exterior cameras—if pictures are going to be taken."

"If?" Miller cocked his head to look at her. "What are you thinking? Won't we definitely want pictures?"

"If we see something. But how gullible we can be sometimes. What if this whole thing's a figment of our imagination?"

Mark lowered his head. "What I saw," he said softly, "was not a figment of my imagination."

Elizabeth quickly turned to him and put a hand on his arm. "Of course not, Mark, forgive me. I didn't really mean you. But I was thinking of those people who claimed they saw those divers being pulled overboard, and the stain and all that."

"I don't know about the divers," Mark said, "or what those two people saw. But the stain will burn your skin if it touches you. I dove near some of it, when I left the speedboat to enter the trench. I could sense that it would burn the skin."

"Well, they were right about that anyway, then," Miller said, nodding.

"And the markings in the trench, I was right about that."

"Of course."

"So if we do not need the cameras, it will only be because you cannot find again what I already found once." Mark smiled slightly.

"Touché, Mark," Miller said, grinning.

There were no houses near this isolated stretch of beach. It was seldom visited by swimmers or beach-combers who, along this part of the Southern California coast, had many more accessible places where they could enjoy the sun, the water, or what the waves cast up. Pieces of gnarled, sun-bleached drift-wood were scattered below the cliffs at the high-tide line, along with an occasional dead fish or shark decaying in the air, pieces of crates, segments of fishing line or hawser. Sandpipers skittered here and there along the lips of the waves. Sand crabs darted back and forth, disappearing into tiny holes, emerging from others. Herring gulls swept the crests of the rollers that beat their way toward the beach.

Day after day this scene was unchanging; nothing disturbed the rhythms of the shoreline solitude.

But on this afternoon, the gulls suddenly wheeled away from the waves, screeching warnings to each other. The sandpipers dashed off down the beach.

Two figures abruptly emerged from the surf and cautiously plodded toward the shore. A man and woman, they were dressed in wetsuits and looked exactly like the vanished divers, Chazz and Dilly. They looked left and then right as they worked their way up onto the beach, slogging through the last fringes of the waves.

The beach seemed alien to them, and they scanned it carefully as if the landscape into which they dared to venture were threatening and forbidding.

Though they appeared together and walked onto the sand side by side, they exchanged no touch or look. They walked heavily, as if the territory were not only new to them, but difficult to traverse as well. They plodded higher onto the sand, then stopped.

They turned their backs to each other and looked long and hard in opposite directions down the expanse of sand and cliffs. Then they walked over to the base of the sandy, crumbling cliffs and along it, looking up at the sheer drop.

When they came to a washed-out path that sloped up through the cliffs, they turned into it. Using their hands to grasp the gnarled roots of bushes, they pulled themselves up between the sandy walls.

The footprints they left in the sand were identifiably those of the neoprene rubber diving slippers they wore. But the handprints where they occasionally balanced themselves during the climb, if examined by an expert, would reveal an unfamiliar pattern.

For the marks showed that their hands were webbed.

chapter 3

The cliffs rose thirty feet, and at the top a hundred yards of knifegrass and brambles stretched before them. Beyond that, a cyclone fence, ten feet tall, extended into the distance in either direction. The fence protected wildlife from the highway, a ribbon of asphalt forlorn except for a small farmhouse surrounded by truck-garden pots.

The two wetsuited figures scrambled over the ledge, rose, looked around, and headed slowly toward the fence. They stopped and examined the steel network from a distance of some yards, slowly turning their heads back and forth. The woman, strangely pretty with long, blond hair, stood slightly behind the man, tall, lean, with piercing gray eyes.

At last they fixed their gaze on a spot to their right, where there was a gate held fast by a huge padlock.

They moved slowly to the gate and studied it. The woman cautiously extended her hands and looped her fingers through the holes in the fence. She tensed her grip and pulled at the thick wire, causing it to flex.

The man tentatively fingered the lock, running his hands over it, pulling it to either side.

Their examinations were not frantic, but deliberate;

yet the gate would not yield to their subtle maneuvers.

They looked at each other, and the man nodded toward the lock. He reached out his hand to her. She stepped close beside him, took his left hand in her right, and clasped it firmly. Then the man put the fingers of his right hand on one side of the lock; she put her left-hand fingers along the other side.

Instantly when they both touched the lock, crackling yellow and blue sparks arced across it, a veritable miniature lightning bolt, sizzling around the forged steel, causing it to glow, smoke, and finally part as if burned through by a blowtorch.

The man nodded and stepped back. The woman removed the severed lock from the gate and swung it open.

"Hey! Hey you two!"

A man in overalls and a straw hat came trotting from the house, waving his arms. "What do you think you're doing with my fence! I'm gonna call the cops!"

They stood staring at him as he ran up.

"You can't come in here! Get out! It cost me a bundle to put up this fence! You surfers drive me crazy! Out! Out!"

He shoved his hand against the strange man's wetsuit, and tried to push him back. The man stiffened and thrust his body against the force of the hand.

The farmer lunged against him. "Out! Out, both of you!"

The man held out his hand to the woman and nodded. She took his hand quickly. They both reached for the farmer, touching their hands to each of his shoulders.

Crackling sparks flew again, and the farmer

slumped to the ground like a rag doll, where he lay crumpled, unconscious but still breathing.

The man and woman advanced quickly through the gate and moved off toward the highway. They stepped onto it, then jumped back off. They looked down at the shimmering asphalt, made hot and soft and sticky by the sun.

They looked up and down the road. In the distance to their left, two church spires and a tall Exxon sign rose over the horizon. The man nodded in that direction.

Side by side they began walking toward the town, their feet moving in a slightly rolling, awkward gait along the stones of the highway shoulder.

A trailer truck approached them from the rear, the roar of its diesel coming upon them suddenly.

They scrambled off into the weeds and remained there, crouched and holding hands, their eyes never leaving the roaring semi until it was a small dot entering the town.

The man nodded to the woman. They unclasped hands and resumed their trek, continually glancing back over their shoulders, watching for other traffic.

Elizabeth and Miller had gone into the rear sphere of the submersible. She bent over to stare into an array of small beakers of sea water on the lab table. Two wires led from a wall console into each of the beakers. She checked the gauges on the console.

"I'm getting a positive readout, Miller. But what does it mean?"

"What kind of readout?" He was reading thermometers he had just taken from the beakers.

"The water seems charged. Resistance is dropping about one or two ohms per five kilometers."

"That's weird."

"What are you getting?"

"Nothing particular. Normal temps. Just what you'd expect around here. Fine for swimming or diving. Oughta be good for tuna. You might think that electrical resistance would affect the temperature."

"Yeah, I know." She leaned over to a microphone and pushed the *Talk* button. "Mark, you see anything yet?"

Mark was in the second sphere, keeping an eye on the bank of television monitors. "No. Nothing yet," his voice came over the speaker. "If our course and estimates are correct, I should see something soon."

"Yeah, right." Elizabeth went back to the beakers. "Resistance still dropping, Miller."

"Hmm, interesting. All of a sudden I'm getting a slight temp fluctuation."

"Something is happening, out there."

"Or happened."

"Yeah."

The intercom rasped with the captain's voice. "Dr. Merrill, there's a call for you from the F.O.R. lab."

"I'll take it on the squawk box."

"Roger."

The box clicked on. Elizabeth sat down next to it. "This is Dr. Merrill. Go ahead, F.O.R."

"Dr. Merrill," came Joe Foley's confident, friendly voice, "one of those three missing people was found washed ashore, and the P.D. message I monitored said the body had some strange markings on it."

Elizabeth paused and looked off at the wall. Then she leaned back to the box. "Call the police, Joe. Tell them that the Foundation has an interest in that body, and we would like to have a look at it."

"Will do. The P.D. is probably gonna ask why. Should I try to finesse it or something?"

"No need, Joe. Just tell them we're already involved in the case, with the Coast Guard."

"Got it. Anything else?"

"Hold on." She looked around at Miller. "Anything?"

He shook his head.

"That's all, Joe. Thanks."

"You bet. This is Fox Oboe Roger. Out."

She swiveled around on the chair. "So, what do you think?"

Miller shrugged. "I try not to think until I can see something to think about."

"Yeah. Maybe we should get some more water samples."

"Okay."

"Captain?" They heard Mark's voice over the intercom. Then some mumbled conversation.

Then the captain's voice came over clear. "Dr. Merrill? Wes here. Mark has something on the monitors. Punch up video four on your monitor in there."

"Roger, Wes." Elizabeth leaned over and pushed the button. The screen lit up. The bow camera panned along the canyon wall, then fixed on one spot ahead and slightly off starboard. The burn slash was visible.

"I see it, Wes." She motioned for Miller to look at the monitor. "Full stop, please."

"All engines stop!" Wes barked.

The humming of engines faded.

"Mark—"

"I'm going to the main airlock," Mark said quickly.
The sub continued to glide slowly forward.

"Let's hold it right here, Wes."

"All engines back one-third!"

The hum rose again.

"Okay. All engines stop! That's it, Dr. Merrill. We're
hovering."

"Thanks, Wes. Mark, we're coming in."

Elizabeth and Miller quickly left their sphere and
ducked through the bulkhead into the second sphere
where Mark was waiting to enter the airlock. He had
removed his jacket, and stood calmly in his swim
trunks which bore the mysterious conch-and-wave
emblem. The airlock man was checking pressures on
the control panel.

"You're all set, Mark?" Elizabeth said, striding over
to him. "We'd better hold our position here just in
case. This contraption would scare anybody."

"Or anything," Mark said.

"Airlock ready for entry," announced the man at
the controls.

"Mark—"

"I know," Mark said at once, with a slight edge in
his voice. "I'll be careful. For you, I have sewn the
blip-signal crystal into my trunks."

He traced his fingers around a small lump in the
waistband.

"Remember," she said, "the range of that is only two
kilometers."

Mark did not respond. He stepped to the airlock
door.

"Mark, I'm not overreacting. It's just that we don't
know what you're going to run into."

Miller stepped forward. "We just want to make sure everything's—"

"You forget." Mark turned to face them. "The sea is my home."

With that he pulled open the airlock door and stepped inside. The control man closed the door behind him and spun the pressure wheel to seal it. He stepped back to his board and manipulated the levers.

Elizabeth and Miller listened to the hiss of escaping air and the rush of entering sea water as the lock was filled.

Miller stared thoughtfully at the sealed door. "Something bugging him lately?"

"Mark?" Elizabeth raised her eyebrows. "What do you mean?"

"He just seems a bit edgy. If it's possible for him to be so, I would say he seems irritable."

"Really? I hadn't noticed. Maybe he just doesn't like to be clucked over so much, as if we didn't entirely trust his judgment."

"Do we?" His question was more a reflective pause than an expression of doubt. But Miller saw the flash of Elizabeth's eyes and immediately added, "Of course we do. I'm sorry. I guess it just strikes me that ever since this thing started he's seemed a little preoccupied."

"He's got a job to do," she said coolly.

"Yes, of course."

When the airlock was filled with water, and its pressure thereby balanced with that of the surrounding sea, Mark easily opened the outer door and slid into the ocean. He stretched and flexed his muscles much as if he had just awakened from sleep, then he executed some aquatic calisthenics—turning, tumbling, generally loosening up.

Then he stopped and hovered in the water. He took a long look around, surveying his immediate surroundings.

Finally he kicked his legs out behind him, angled his body down and forward, in the same direction the submersible had been heading. He quickly picked up the first traces of the burn on the canyon wall.

The man and woman in wetsuits trudged warily into the town, swiveling their heads slowly back and forth like patroling searchlights. To the casual eye, they were not unusual; surfers and divers strolling the streets in wetsuits were not an uncommon sight in this seacoast village. The townspeople had a tolerance for visitors from the beach who often came there to rent rooms or buy equipment or eat meals; surfers and divers were seldom without hard cash. The only annoyance these visitors caused—aside from an occasional squabble over prices—was when they sat in a booth or on a stool in wetsuits which were still wet. But even then, a quick, tidying swipe with a dry rag was well worth the profits they brought in.

The man and woman now entering the town were not relaxed. They kept their hands fisted to conceal the webbing—which they quickly saw would set them noticeably apart from others. And their searching eyes were intent on absorbing styles and manners, which they quickly learned and copied. Pedestrians crossed the streets only when the lights facing them were green; this pair did the same. Pedestrians stopped here and there to look into shop windows; these two did likewise. Some couples nodded or shook their heads in conversation; this couple did so too, except that they didn't talk. But unlike those occasional pairs who ambled along hand and hand, these two did not touch.

All in all, they were convincing enough to draw no particular attention, which was, of course, their primary hope.

They came to a corner and waited for the light to change. A man came up and stood beside them, a curved pipe dangling from his mouth. The man took from his pocket a silver Nimrod Pipeliter and flicked it alive, sending a tiny torch of flame into the air.

The pair ducked quickly away, their eyes wide with terror. Instantly they locked hands.

The man with the lighter, startled by their movements, blinked at them. "Sorry," he said with a puzzled smile.

The pair exchanged a look and dropped hands. "Yes," the woman said.

The man turned away from them, lit his pipe, and proceeded across the street.

The couple waited for him to advance, then they also stepped off the curb. But the light had just then changed. A Corvette Stingray gunned its engine impatiently. The pair spun around toward the roar, locked hands, then raced for the far curb. They stood for a few moments breathing heavily and looking around. But they didn't stand still long. For one thing they noticed above all else was that people on these streets kept moving.

They proceeded down the sidewalk behind a group of laughing teenagers in swimsuits and rubber sandles.

* * *

Mark continued into the trench at moderate speed, swimming with his undulating, eely motion, scanning the canyon walls as he went. On his right, a black scar paralleled his path along the mountainlike terrain. He swam close to it, fixing his gaze on it. He began to move his lips as if in speech.

Inside the submersible, Mark's lip movements caused the radio operator suddenly to smile broadly and smack his fist into his palm. "It's working! UNDER's picking him up! I've got voice contact!"

It was his pride and joy. The radio operator, Robert K. Brown—called "Bobby-K"—had, for most of his career prior to joining the F.O.R. staff, been an unappreciated genius. He was always tinkering with standard communications gear to adapt it to do special and unusual things. He had once been fired from the Detroit Police Department for so successfully altering the radio there that it picked up an emergency call in Cleveland. Unfortunately, prowl cars from his own department attempted to respond, there being similar Oak Street addresses in both Detroit and Cleveland.

For the submersible, he had rather modestly suggested that he might adapt the boat's system to be able to pick up a voice deep in the sea. Such an adaptation—if it worked, and at first no one but him had supposed it might—would be useful only to Mark Harris, for no ordinary mortal human being could speak normally several hundred feet beneath the surface of the sea. Of course scuba divers could carry tiny voice transmitters in their face masks. But Mark wore no such thing. To be able to communicate with him as he explored the depths would be an enormous advantage.

Bobby-K had tinkered and adjusted for months, encouraged only by Joe Foley, the radio man back at F.O.R. He finally thought he had done it, and asked Mark to try it out on this trip.

Now he squirmed ecstatically in his chair. "Captain," he said excitedly, "I am picking up the voice of Mark Harris on the Ultra-high-frequency Neutronic Directional Responder. Dr. Merrill can talk to him if she'd like to punch up the 'B' system."

Wes looked stunned for an instant, then nodded and pushed the microphone button. "Dr. Merrill? Bobby-K has Mark on UNDER. Take it on the 'B' board."

Elizabeth and Miller had been watching on the monitor the sonar blip from the quartz unit in Mark's trunks. When they heard the captain's announcement, their mouths dropped open and they stared at each other. While they had been fretting about him out there, Mark had coolly surprised them by remembering to try the UNDER system. In their fretting, they had forgotten it was to be tried.

For a moment Elizabeth wondered whether Mark had purposefully planned to go them one-up, by calmly employing science while they, in their doubt and nervousness, were unprepared.

But quickly she squared her shoulders and regained her professional demeanor. She slid over and punched up the "B" board. "Yes, Mark?"

"I see it," came his voice, disguised by strange modulations that resulted from filtration through the sea. "I am tracing the markings on the rock."

"We read you," Elizabeth said, smiling over at Miller whose mouth was still agape.

"The burn is about one meter wide," Mark went on, his words separated by soft gurglings. "The descent angle is forty degrees. It appears to have vaporized everything on the face of the rock within about six meters of its center. I will continue to follow it."

Mark moved along the face of the rock, occasionally running his hands over the markings. He dropped deeper and deeper into the trench. To an ordinary diver without a light, everything at this depth would have been in blackness. But Mark's brilliant green eyes saw clearly. The pressures of such depth did not affect him, nor the temperatures, which would have chilled a scuba man quickly. He was entirely at home in that environment, even though the particular site he was examining was new and alien.

"I am approaching the floor of the trench," he said into the sea.

As he dropped down toward the sandy floor, he suddenly stopped. He hovered, looking down, then began slowly circling. "I see something on the floor." He spiraled slowly down.

Protruding from the seabed was a large, angular, silvery tube, like a rectangular funnel, with one end buried, the other end slanting up about three meters from the bottom. The outer rim of the opening was about two meters across, and the narrowing corridor leading down inside it was darker even than the dark sea.

"I see a large open metallic tube embedded in the floor," Mark said. He swam slowly around it, eying it up and down, drawn ever closer to the yawning opening.

He swam over it, then stopped and hovered, staring down into the mouth of the funnel.

At last he said briskly, "I'm going in."

Without waiting for a reply, he plunged down into the tube.

"How deep is he?" Miller asked into the intercom.

"Two thousand, one hundred meters," the second officer, seated before the sonar console, replied evenly. "We just lost the blip."

The captain sprang to Bobby-K's side. "Will you be able to pick him up in there?" he asked urgently.

"I don't know, sir. That's a situation I didn't figure on." He strained at the earphones, twisting the dials to full volume.

In the adjoining sphere, Elizabeth stooped over the scanner. She saw the blip flash twice, heard the two corresponding pip-tones. Then the monitor went dark and quiet.

"We've lost him!" she cried, her face sagging. She jumped over to the "B" board. "Bobby-K! Are you getting anything?"

"No, Doctor, afraid not. Sorry."

Elizabeth sat staring at the console.

Miller slid onto the stool beside her. "That doesn't mean anything's wrong," he said softly, trying to console her. "He's just gone inside something."

"Just gone inside something!" Her eyes flashed angrily at him.

"He knows what he's doing, Elizabeth, isn't that so?"

She put her hand over her eyes.

"He's not crazy or wild or suicidal. He's as professional as we are, isn't he?"

She nodded slowly, still covering her eyes.

"If he didn't think it was necessary, he wouldn't be doing it, would he?"

She shook her head.

"So let's just take it easy and wait for him to report, okay?"

She dropped her hand from her eyes and looked at him and sighed. "It's just that sometimes I get the feeling Mark's being *used*, used by us. What does he get out of this, after all? He's not bucking for funds or prestige. Still we ask him to take risks for us."

"Discovery, Elizabeth. He is as inquisitive as we are. If we saw such a tube embedded in the side of a mountain on land, we would want to explore it. The sea is his land. I think he is, at heart, a scientist."

She rubbed a hand slowly across her cheek. "Miller?"

"Yes?"

"Don't try to humor me."

"Okay."

"You're just as worried as I am."

He shrugged. "I try not to worry about things I can't do anything about."

"We sent him down there."

"Against his will? Elizabeth." He put an arm gently around her shoulders. "You are being condescending to our unusual associate. In your mind, you are treating him like a child or a baboon. Down there, Elizabeth, at the bottom of the sea, he is superior to any of us. Let him do the worrying."

She sloughed off his arm. "Such callousness."

"Not callousness, Doctor, realism. Perhaps he will make a discovery to excite us all."

"Or perhaps he'll disappear."

"Perhaps that, too."

* * *

Mark swam headfirst down through the tube and emerged into a single, large, water-filled chamber.

The walls, ceiling, and floor of this room were a jumble of clashing, angular, shiny surfaces which would, in daylight, have created a series of fun-house reflections.

Mark landed on his feet and began to prowl through this watery domain. Because of the pattern and course of the burn scar on the granite of the trench, this clearly was the craft that caused it. And because of its location, it clearly was this same craft that left the fiery trail in the sky that the Meteorological Bureau had observed.

So it came from somewhere in space, to land here in the sea. And though there were no chairs or bunks or tables or desks that would suggest the quarters of a crew, still it was meant for habitation, however brief. At one end of the room was a bank of control levers, labeled with visual symbols. One label showing a puff of smoke could be the power switch. Others showing directional arrows were perhaps the craft's altitude controls. Some labels seemed to be indicators of various atmospheric conditions. In the center of the bank was a sort of clock whose markings were not hours but signs of the zodiac.

Mark studied all these labels and levers and dials closely. He stared at one label that displayed a glittering, fountainlike spray. Lightly he put his hand on the corresponding lever, paused, then slowly pulled it down.

At once the compartment was filled with an atonal but strangely soothing, tinkly kind of music.

He pushed the lever back up, the music ceased.

He pulled another lever labeled with an emblem of

the sun, and the cabin was then bathed in a subdued, diffused light, the source of which he could not detect.

He backed away from the control board and began walking around the angular room, looking at the multiplicity of facets and bevels of pristine metal that surrounded him. The effect of the light reflecting from the surfaces, and being re-reflected from a hundred different metallic faces, was dizzying, and Mark found himself swaying as he walked. The shiny surfaces made the room seem larger than it was. He could detect no exits from the room save the tube through which he had entered, no doors or sliding panels or portholes. Apparently the craft consisted of just this one bare chamber.

Bedazzled by all the strange angles, Mark did not notice the large, glasslike box in one corner until he almost bumped into it. This box stood about his height, a meter wide and half a meter deep, transparent and empty. The full-length door was hinged at the top. Something in the hinges caught his eye.

Several dark filaments were enmeshed in the hinges as if they had been caught there.

But they were not firmly stuck, and Mark easily pulled them out and looked at them. To him they seemed like human hairs. He stuck them under the waistband of his trunks.

He turned and scanned the room. In an opposite corner, there was something on the floor that had escaped his attention earlier. He walked over and knelt beside it.

It seemed to be a broken piece of something opaque, like a clay tile. Gingerly he picked up the shard, about half the size of his palm. There was a design on it. He turned it around.

Suddenly he stood up. He held the shard against the leg of his trunks.

The design on the shard was nearly the same—a spiral shell over a row of tiny waves. It was not an exact duplicate of the symbol on his trunks—it was like what someone might have drawn from memory after briefly seeing his emblem. The colors were different. His emblem was blue, this one was black.

But the resemblance triggered something in him and he stared at the shard and knit his brows in thought. As he stood there, his stare became increasingly vacant, as if he were lost in some very distant memory. He stood rapt for several minutes.

Then he shook his head as if to clear it, knelt, and replaced the shard exactly as he had found it.

Among things lacking in this chamber, things that might lead to some recognition or suggestion as to where it came from and who came in it, were any kind of papers, logs, documents—materials to indicate its business.

And so once again Mark went slowly along the walls, searching for anything that might be a clue.

He came upon two pale red buttons, the size of a thumb tip, about chest high on a wall. They were lodged in the opposite ends of a six-inch groove, and were separated by a black bar whose end-notches were locked onto each button and would prevent their sliding together in the groove.

And yet it looked to Mark as if there were something very significant in their sliding together. There was half a design on each of the buttons, and if they were united, the two halves would complete a recognizable scene: a volcano spewing ash and fire.

He had been inside the craft for quite a while. He

moved toward the entry tube. Then he turned and once again surveyed the room, letting his eyes roam very slowly over every detail, as if to fix it firmly in his memory.

Then he dove up into the tube and swam out.

"It's been almost an hour, Miller."

"I know."

"I'm going to try again."

He shrugged.

Elizabeth leaned close to the UNDER mike and spoke loudly and clearly. "Mark, respond if you read me. Respond if you read me." She shook her head. "Nothing."

"Give him time."

"You think we should move the sub in closer?"

"I wouldn't, Elizabeth. But it's your sub to command."

"I don't like you to think of it that way. It's both of ours."

"Okay. I think we should stay here."

A faint gurgling noise came over the UNDER speaker. "I'm now returning," Mark's filtered voice announced.

Startled, then delighted, Elizabeth bent quickly to the mike. "Mark, are you okay? Is everything okay?"

"Everything's okay," he said.

"Whew!" She leaned back and looked at Miller.

Miller smiled.

"Don't be smug!" she snapped.

Then they both laughed in relief.

The two scientists rushed into the other sphere, to the airlock, and stood waiting. The airlock controller waited by his gauges and levers, and checked his wrist chronometer.

In a few moments, Mark's arrival was announced by a soft toot of the Klaxon horn, meaning that he had pushed the button outside the exterior door. The controller pulled a lever, there was a hydraulic hiss, and then the man said, "Exterior door open."

Mark's face appeared in the airlock window.

The controller pulled levers and the pumps pushed the water out of the lock, replacing it with air. He watched the dials on his board. Then he locked the levers in place and stepped to the airlock door. He spun the sealing wheel counterclockwise and pulled the heavy door open.

Mark stepped into the room, still dripping water, and spoke before anyone else could. "I have something remarkable to tell you."

Elizabeth put a hand on his arm. "Are you sure everything's—"

"Please. I must tell you what I saw."

"What?" Miller asked. "Come on, we're anxious."

"I need a pencil. And paper. Please."

A crewman came in cradling a pile of towels in his arms and held them out to Mark. He grabbed the top two, sending a few others wafting to the deck, and began to dry himself hurriedly.

Elizabeth took a white pad and felt-tipped pen from a desk drawer and handed them to him.

Mark finished drying his hands thoroughly, took the pad and pen, hauled the chair out from the desk, sat down, and began to draw. As he sketched the interior of the strange craft, he recounted his discoveries. He turned out a crude drawing of the chamber, recognizable to anyone who might have seen it, but, due to the complexities of the facets of the room, not entirely comprehensible to Elizabeth and Miller.

Nonetheless they nodded.

"That's as much as I can remember," he said, his voice still bearing traces of the urgency he had expressed when he emerged from the air lock. "Oh!" He stuck his fingers under his waistband. "Here's the hairs that I found in the door to the transparent cabinet."

Elizabeth took them and sat down at a lab table before a microscope. She carefully placed two hairs on a glass slide, focused, and studied them.

Miller repeatedly shook his head. "And you say there was music?"

"It was like music. It was different from the music you play in the lab, or any I have ever heard before. It was as if performed by electronic means, very delicate, very peaceful, sometimes like a waterfall, sometimes like the tinkling of crystal glass. It was not music to excite, but to soothe. Perhaps it was something you would have recognized, something you would have a better word for than music. But to me, it was closer to music than anything else I know."

"Fascinating! I'd give anything to visit that room and hear that music!"

"These are not human hairs," Elizabeth said, still bent over her microscope. "They look like human hairs, and even feel like human hairs. But they're not. They aren't plastic hairs, either."

"Well, what are they then?"

"They're made out of something akin to catfish whiskers—a fine, aqueous cartilage."

"Well, catfish didn't drive that thing!" Miller spouted. "It's got to be a spaceship, that's all there is to it!" He bounced energetically around the sphere, tapping a fist into a palm. "A spaceship from a water planet!"

"I don't know if we can make that leap just yet," Elizabeth said, turning from her microscope.

"Yes we can!" Miller beamed with delight.

Elizabeth's manner was much more subdued. "But then who brought it here? Or *what* brought it here?"

Mark studied the floor silently, but Miller hopped happily from one foot to the other.

"It's finally happened!" the scientist exclaimed as he jabbed an index finger into the air. "Beings from outer space have landed! We're at the dawning of the Age of Aquarius! Holy-moly, what a wonderful moment!"

Mark looked at him. "You're not frightened?"

"Scientists don't get frightened, Mark, my boy! They get awed! That's what I am—awed! Awed and excited! As awed and excited as I could possibly be! We are on the edge of the greatest discovery of the century—perhaps since the dawn of man!"

"Miller—"

"Forgive me, Elizabeth." He calmed down quickly, his chest still heaving. "I know you like to take things slow and sure. I couldn't help myself. It's so inspiring!"

"Miller," she said evenly, "it's possible there are three deaths connected with this."

"We don't know that those deaths are connected with this."

"And we don't know they're not!" she snapped, striding to the center of the room. "How do we know if the beings who came in that ship are friendly or hostile? And what do we do about it? We've got a big responsibility! That's what you should be awed about!"

The room lapsed into a heavy-breathing calm. The many varying emotions compressed into a short period of time had so flayed the spirits and brains of Miller, Mark, and Elizabeth that it seemed they all were suddenly bereft of energy. They stood looking at the floor and each other in a room grown heavy with the implications of Mark's discoveries. The walls pressed in on the three, each with a different makeup, a different reference point from which to formulate a course of action.

"All right," Elizabeth said finally, "I'm going to tell C.W. to get in touch with Washington." She started for the phone.

"No!" Mark took a step forward, his palm raised to her. "No! You must not!"

"Why not?"

Miller, stepped up beside Mark, and though for different reasons objected, "Elizabeth, don't you realize what's going on here? Don't you see we're the first people in the world to really experience this? If we act hastily, we could ruin history for all time. We could throw the whole planet into a panic!" He waved his arms. "These beings must be incredible! Look at their technology!"

"We don't know anything about them!" Elizabeth snapped back. "They could be killers!"

"Dr. Merrill?" All heads turned toward the intercom speakers from which came the voice of the captain.

"Yes, Wes."

"Should we head home, or what?"

"Stand by, Wes. I'll tell you in a minute."

"Roger. Standing by."

She reached decisively for the phone and picked it up.

Mark put his hand gently on hers and pushed the receiver back onto its cradle. "They are not here to kill. Give us, all of us, time to understand." He looked over at Miller, who was nodding, then back at Elizabeth, who narrowed her eyes to look at him. "It's very important."

"I know." She gradually withdrew her hand from the phone. "Don't you think I know?"

"I don't mean just what we have discovered, but the time is important."

"My sentiments exactly, Mark. That's why I think Washington should be notified immediately. We don't know how much time we have. I don't think we have the right to take the whole responsibility for this on our own shoulders, for selfish reasons. Too much is at stake."

"I too am concerned, Elizabeth. It is my strong feeling that we can afford to wait a short time. It is not for selfish reasons only. Please."

She appraised him coolly, staring into his deep, green eyes, examining the firm set of his mouth, sensing the strength of his conviction; weighing all this against the waves of urgency that beat within her, the wails of alarm that echoed in her head.

Then she looked over at Miller, absorbing the heated vibrations of his enthusiasm over a new discovery, and considering the bond of their scientific work together, the brilliance and dedication of his mind.

And she felt oddly isolated. Her mighty wish that

they could rejoin in spirit and action suddenly over-whelmed her instincts, made her feel that she had foolishly overreacted.

"All right," she said softly. "We'll give it some time."

chapter 4

The ride home was painfully quiet, each of them immersed in private thoughts. Miller's exuberance had temporarily exhausted him. Elizabeth wrestled inwardly with second and third thoughts. And Mark . . .

"We'll be making the turn into the sub pen in two minutes," Wes announced.

"Would you come in here for a minute, please, Wes?"

"Sure, Dr. Merrill, be right there."

Elizabeth was gathering up notebooks, records, film cans, tape cassettes, and other materials to take ashore when Wes came through the bulkhead.

"Wes," she said quietly, almost whispering, "for the time being, not a word about any of this to anyone." She had, as she felt was proper and necessary, briefed Wes on Mark's discoveries.

"I'll take care of it with the crew," he said soberly.

"Thanks."

"I better get back to the helm."

"Right."

She watched him leave, a man she trusted implicitly. He had left the command of a Navy sub to take this job, because he wanted to run a ship designed for peaceful missions. His casual and pleasant manner with the crew belied his iron will, fierce pride, and stiff self-discipline. His job was to oversee the successful performance of the submersible, and to insure the safety of all those on board—including the scientists. That's why she had shared the information with him. A man with that responsibility should not be ignorant of the facts and implications of the mission.

"Elizabeth," Mark said softly, "you should not be so worried."

She turned to look at him. There was something in those strange green eyes that was not usually there. She thought she had seen it before, when he had returned from the sea, and again, when he had asked her not to use the telephone. And now, it was still there, like a shield. "Mark, is there something you haven't told me?"

He blinked and took a deep breath, but did not answer. He stared directly at her, a look that could be either a challenge to her question or an invitation for her to pursue it.

"Mark, this is serious. You have to tell me everything you know. You have to trust me, like always. Like I must trust you. It is the only way we can work together."

"They . . . they are . . ." his voice was stiff, as if stuck between his teeth, "my people. They . . . have come for me."

Miller spun around to look at him, but said nothing.

"Why?" Elizabeth asked breathlessly. "What makes you think that?"

Mark's hesitant words tumbled like nuggets. "I didn't tell you before. Something I found—on the floor of that spacecraft—told me this truth."

"What thing?" Elizabeth groped behind her for a chair and started to sit down, but immediately straightened up again. "What thing did you find?"

He looked down at the symbol on the leg of his trunks and traced his finger slowly around its edges. "I found a piece of hard material, like clay. On it was . . . this same design."

Now Elizabeth sank slowly into the chair. She rubbed one temple with her hand. "But Mark, you don't even know what that symbol means. You don't know where it comes from."

"It comes from my people." He looked down at her. The reserve was gone from his eyes. "I am sure."

Miller took a seat also, and rubbed a hand slowly and harshly back and forth over his chin.

Mark looked from one set of wide eyes to the other.

The sub edged in between the pilings of its pen, and nestled against the dock.

Mark left the two scientists sitting in silence to go aft to get his jacket.

C.W. Crawford, Jr., liked to admire such a fine day. Dressed in an elegant three-piece pinstripe suit, carrying an expensive leather briefcase with a combination lock, he stopped at the main door of the F.O.R. building to smooth the gray hair over his temples and to admire the day. He was one of those men who loved to stop and grant nature a brief audience, give her a token of his appreciation, just before hurrying indoors.

Once inside the F.O.R. building, he hurried through the corridor in the direction of the closed door to the main lab.

Ginny looked up as he approached.

He waved jauntily and moved right past her desk.

"How's the most beautiful girl in the Foundation to-day?" he said over his shoulder.

"You said that to Dr. Merrill yesterday."

"Yesterday she was," he said, turning to Ginny and putting a hand on the lab doorknob. "Today you are."

"No point in going in there," she said pleasantly.

"No point in going in there?"

She shook her head, smiling.

He ran a manicured hand down the side of his jacket. "I'm supposed to administer a twelve-million-dollar budget for this place," he said, sulkily, "and I'm not even supposed to go into the lab? How come, Ginny? Miller got a card game going on in there?"

"Oh sure." She chuckled. "He usually plays two ta-bles of bridge with the laboratory octopus about this time."

He frowned. "Very funny. You don't want me going in there because—" he suddenly turned the knob and swung the door open "—they're out joyriding in the sub again!"

Ginny blushed. "They'll be back any minute."

Crawford fumed, and looked as if he wanted to stomp his foot. "I knew it!" He did stomp his foot, both feet, but he slammed one down in front of the other so that it became a walk rather than a tantrum. He stomped into the lab and stomped back out. "They've exceeded their allocation again! We haven't got the money for it! We're funded, you know, we're not some operation running on private profits! We're on a tight budget! What am I supposed to do? Wait until the bills come in and then say I'm sorry, we won't pay?" He stomped over to her desk. "Hunh?"

"I don't know, Mr. Crawford."

"Of course not," he hissed, "you're just the secretary."

She straightened up and looked at him with half-closed eyes and a wry smile. "I believe you said I was the most beautiful girl in the Foundation."

"Hmph."

"In any event," she turned back to her typewriter, "I'm sure they'll be happy to see you, when they get back." She thought she could hear a faint gnashing of his teeth.

He stomped back into the lab and around it as if expecting to find the two scientists lurking behind an aquarium. Then he stomped out and went over to the elevator and jabbed a thumb at the button, missing it, annoyingly, on the first try, and breaking his nail, distressingly, on the second successful one.

The crew and scientists were just debarking the sub when Crawford strolled into the pen. He had regained his earlier reserved but hearty demeanor.

Elizabeth walked onto the dock, followed by Mark and Miller.

"Well, glad you're back," Crawford said, smiling. "I think maybe we should all go into the conference room for a little coffee and tête-à-tête, hmm?"

Without breaking stride, they filed silently past him.

He quickly brought up the rear. "Tea? Rather have tea?"

They headed for the tunnel door.

"Aha!" He held up a finger. "Grog! We'll break out the tumblers to welcome back the returning voyagers!"

Still no response. He trotted behind them. "Look, let's be serious."

They entered the tunnel and kept walking. "So," he said, nodding briskly, "no one is talking to me. Well, either you had a voyage that was a total failure, or, heh-heh, I am personally so repulsive that no one wishes to share a word with me."

"How about a teeny-weeny touch of both?" Elizabeth said over her shoulder.

"I wish you hadn't said that," Crawford said, glad she couldn't see his face flush. "I keep hoping that one of these days there'll be a light in your eyes that says you care."

He listened for her retort—expecting nothing comforting, just something that would at least keep the conversation alive. He heard nothing.

He tried another tack. "Well, Mark Harris. Hi there. How are you?"

"Fine, C.W." Politely, he slowed a bit, to allow Crawford to walk beside him.

Encouraged, Crawford raised his voice. "It costs us approximately fifteen thousand dollars every time that submersible goes out, and—"

"C. W." Elizabeth suddenly stopped and turned toward him. "Can't we get into this with you later?"

"No," he huffed, folding his arms over his chest.

"Can't you see that Elizabeth doesn't want to talk just now?" Miller said, stepping beside her. "Isn't that enough for you?"

"Among other things," Crawford said, pacing back and forth in front of them, pleased that he had finally succeeded in making them stop, "I have to talk to you about national defense. And Mark, the Navy wants you involved."

Mark glanced at Elizabeth.

"Old buddy," Crawford continued, putting an officious hand on Mark's shoulder, "you're here now, not wherever you came from. Don't tell me there's no national defense where you came from because you don't know where you came from and maybe there *is* national defense there. And it is my belief there is, if they've got any pride in country, any backbone, any sense of honor and—"

"We can't stop for this now," Elizabeth said firmly. "There's an evaluation that we have to make immediately."

"Of what?" He asked the question only to compensate for the unwelcomed interruption.

"There's a body at the morgue in town. It washed ashore at Lincoln Beach this morning."

"Now, Elizabeth, what has that got to do with—"

"The Coast Guard has asked us to relate it to a dye stain they found in the water." Her voice was filled with authority.

"Well, if it's the Coast Guard, then of course you have to go . . ." Crawford trailed off.

They hurried on through the tunnel and entered the elevator, leaving Crawford alone, scuffing his toe in chagrin.

"Nice going," Miller said.

"Thanks."

"I've gotta hand it to you, my dear Miss Elizabeth, you really know when to assert yourself."

"And when to cry?" She smiled ironically at him.

He chuckled, then turned sober. "Can you imagine his hysteria if he knew what we were thinking about?"

"What did he mean, about national defense?" Mark asked, looking at Elizabeth.

"Don't worry, Mark. Whatever it is, you know the arrangement. They have to get approval from you *and*

me before they can give you a military assignment.
How we avoid it is to keep very busy on important
work of our own. And I think we can all agree that we
are so occupied, at present."

Mark nodded. Miller smiled. Elizabeth rubbed a
hand over her eyes and sighed.

The two figures in wetsuits had traversed the entire downtown area of the seacoast community, and if
they were to attract any attention now it would come
from someone who had watched them from the beginning, and seen that their wanderings were hesitant
and aimless. In fact, despite their attempts to appear
casual, the two were growing ever more nervous and
edgy; their stride was quicker, the flicking left and
right of their eyes was more frantic, their hands were
more tightly clenched.

They came upon a place they had passed earlier,
when first entering the town. This time they stopped.

It was a seafood restaurant and store, with an out-
door café where people clustered around small, white
tables under large, orange umbrellas. Lunchers ate
mounds of iced shrimp cocktail or planks of pink
salmon or white flounder.

The couple maneuvered among the tables to stand
at the broad window filled with crates of ice which
made beds for all sorts of seafood. They stared at the
fish. They looked around at the diners, fixing their
gaze particularly on those who were using knives and
forks to pry meat from the shells of lobsters and crabs.
Then they looked back into the display case.

A low whine came from the woman's mouth, then a
wavering cry.

The man looked at her sharply. "Speak as they speak," he muttered.

"I need nourishment," she said, following those words with another plaintive sound.

"Yes." He pointed to the door of the store, and they went in. They surveyed the customers and the decor: nets and floats, plastic swordfish and pictures of fishermen adorned the walls; people waited at the service counter while clerks wrapped up parcels of limp fish and hard clams. A clerk held up two fish by their tails, a man and woman looked at them, then the woman pointed to the larger of the fish and the clerk slapped it down on the counter for wrapping. Waiters bustled through, balancing trays of steaming plates of fish for the tables outside, or trays heaped with dirty plates for the dishwasher.

The woman in the wetsuit leaned close to her companion. "Do you see the young one eating with the adults?" She nodded toward a table occupied by a family; the mother was cutting up tiny bits of fish and feeding them to a child in a high chair.

"I see," he said, "yes. And the food. They eat it dead. How do they kill it? And when? When do they kill this food we see lying all around us, food that lived in the sea and is now dead?"

They edged closer to the counter to watch a clerk wrapping a handful of gray eels. The clerk folded them in waxy brown paper, and after deftly knotting a length of string around the package, handed it to a waiting customer. Then he turned to the wetsuited couple.

"Can I help you with something?"

The man in the wetsuit stepped back, staring, then

approached the counter, uncertainly. "How do you kill them?" he asked in a low voice. "With poison?"

The clerk chuckled. "With kindness. Yes sir, kill 'em with kindness. That's the motto of Bait 'n Bite. What'll it be?"

"Yes," said the man in the wetsuit. He looked around. On the end of the counter stood an aquarium with four live fish hovering in the water. Seaweed fluttered at the bottom of the tank. "There. In that case." He nodded toward it, not exposing his hand.

"Here?" The clerk moved down to the aquarium, patted the side, and gestured toward the fish, naturally assuming that was what the man in the wetsuit had in mind. "They're prize carp, mister. Worth about two hundred clams apiece. Not for sale."

"Two hundred clams." The man looked at the case thoughtfully. "But the seaweed. How many clams is the seaweed worth?"

The clerk laughed. "Oh yeah, that stuff's *really* expensive. Say, you folks just come in here to tease me and brighten my day, or can I help you with something? Some fine, fresh fish?"

The couple stepped away from the counter. "Clams," said the man to the woman, "are a unit of exchange here."

"The computer evidently did not absorb that. We have no clams."

"No."

The clerk continued to stare at them, and they glanced at him and moved away out the door.

Still glancing back at the clerk and the display window, the man bumped the arm of a waitress carrying a pot of coffee. Coffee splashed out of the pot onto the arm of his wetsuit.

He gasped loudly as if in intense pain, causing the diners to turn toward him.

"Sorry, sir," the waitress said, quickly putting down the pot and taking a clean cloth napkin from a table, "I'm really sorry. Here, let me wipe that off for you."

The man moaned and closed his eyes as she took his arm with one hand and wiped it off with the napkin. "Probably be good to rinse out your suit when you get home. Coffee's pretty acidy, might eat a hole in the neoprene." Suddenly she stopped wiping and looked at the arm that she held in her hand. "Why . . ." she looked puzzled, "this feels like skin."

The man yanked his arm free, and he and the woman trotted away through the tables and across the street.

When they had rounded a corner and were out of view of the restaurant, she asked, "The pain? Has it gone? Are you satisfactory?"

"I am satisfactory. Let us continue walking. It is not good to stand still on these streets." They resumed their walk. "What of you? Are you satisfactory?"

"I need nourishment."

"Yes. We both need nourishment."

They stopped and looked around.

"Yes," the man said. "Nourishment. Come. We will go back to where the people were eating. You will have nourishment."

They retraced their steps and crossed the street to the restaurant. They stood looking at the tables.

"Come," he said.

She followed him into the store. They walked briskly to the aquarium at the end of the counter. They looked at the two clerks down the counter from them. Both were busy wrapping fish.

While her companion stood between her and the clerks, she suddenly dipped her hand into the tank, ripped out a hunk of seaweed, whirled, and headed for the door.

"Hey! Hey there, you two! What're you doing with my kelp? Hey! Stop!"

They ran out, darted across the street between cars, turned a corner, and disappeared down an alley.

The white-jacketed assistant medical examiner led Elizabeth, Miller, and Mark down a corridor toward the morgue. "Oh, we get all kinds of strange ones. That's what makes this job interesting. You wouldn't believe how many ways people could find to bite the dust. I'm telling you. We see them all. Right in here, please."

He ushered them into the morgue, a bright room of enamel and steel, spotless and odorless. One wall was made up entirely of large drawers, like a giant built-in file cabinet.

"Right over here." He pulled one of the drawers out, bringing it forward several feet into the room. "This is the one. His name is Herbert Wayman. Age, forty-five. Occupation, plumbing contractor. One of the three sport divers reported missing. The other two haven't shown up yet. But they will. Eventually, like as not, they'll be brought in here."

Elizabeth stooped over to observe one of the dead man's hands. Most of it was stained purple. There was a definite waterline mark; the stain covered all the fingers and ended on a diagonal halfway between the knuckles and the wrist. In addition to being stained, the skin seemed sered, as if burned.

"What do you make of the stain?" she asked.

"Whatever it is," said the A.M.E., shaking his head, "we've never seen it before. Don't know whether it's acid or base, and why it didn't dilute in water. It burns like an acid, apparently, but it's not nitric, formic, sulfuric, hydrochloric, citric, or anything else familiar. We were hoping you might know."

"We don't. We had samples, but they've deteriorated."

"Well, we didn't go into it too deeply, because that stain or burn or whatever isn't what killed him."

"What *was* the cause of death?" Miller asked. "Drowning, I assume?"

"Well, there was water in the lungs." The A.M.E. rubbed his chin thoughtfully. "But there's also an indication of electrocution."

"Electrocution?" Miller wrinkled up his eyes.

"Except that there are no contact burns on the exterior. We've got the guy's cousin or uncle or something coming up here tomorrow. If he'll sign for an autopsy, maybe we can figure something out."

"How much voltage?" Miller asked, staring down at the body.

"Voltage where?"

"You said electrocution."

"Oh, that. Yeah. We don't know. Enough to make him dead. Beyond that we don't know. You can't get deader than dead."

A radio call came over the loudspeaker. "Eighteen-A-six, over."

Mark stepped up and leaned over to examine the stained hand.

"Don't touch," the A.M.E. said.

"No."

The A.M.E. shrugged. "Not that there's anything

wrong with it, really. But that's the rule, you know? Far as I'm concerned, you could handle him like a masseur, you know. But that's the rule. Something about insurance or something."

"Go ahead, Eighteen-A-six," came a woman's voice over the P.A.

"On tag thirty-six, Mary, you said petty theft? I'll say it was petty. You know what was stolen? Some seaweed out of a fish tank. And the chick who stole it, ate it!"

Elizabeth looked over at the P.A. speaker. "What are we listening to?"

"Oh, some police car beefing about a call he got," the A.M.E. said. "We listen in to get the dead-body calls."

"Anyhow, Mary," continued the police call, "she and her boyfriend were in wetsuits and I spotted them around Second and Greene, but then I got an armed robbery. I'm glad I did. I didn't want to book her for eating stolen seaweed. I never would have heard the end of it."

The female voice giggled. "I understand, Eighteen-A-six. How can I clear it?"

"Clear it as a reported four-eighty-eight, petty theft, kelp—no evidence."

"Okay, Eighteen-A-six. Dispatcher out."

Mark had suddenly tensed, and Elizabeth and Miller noticed it and looked at him.

"Something about that call, Mark?" Elizabeth asked.

"Yes."

"You two go ahead. I want to go over the M.E. report on this."

Miller and Mark hurriedly left the room and went out to Miller's car.

"About that police call, Mark?"

"Yes," Mark said, sliding into the passenger side.

"You're thinking about that . . . eating the seaweed."

"Yes."

"Could be just a gag, hunh?"

"Then I would like to find the two who stole the seaweed and see if they are laughing."

They had to drive only a few minutes before Miller stopped the car. "This is Second and Greene," he said, sliding out of the driver's side. "We're looking for a couple in wetsuits. I guess that's all we've got to go on. Apparently otherwise they're just like us."

"Us?" Mark said, slamming the door. "You and I are not the same."

"Don't be so touchy, Mr. Harris," Miller said, smiling warmly. "You know what I mean."

"Yes. Let us separate. You look over there, around the central area. I will search toward the canal."

Miller came around the car and looked closely at Mark's face. "Mark, I think maybe you've been out of the water about as long as you should be—almost fourteen hours. You're going to need to get wet soon."

"Yes, but I'm still all right. I'm sure I can last a few hours more."

"Maybe. But we'll meet back here in thirty minutes anyway. Okay?" He held out his wrist and tapped his watch. "Half an hour should be enough. If we don't find them by then, they're gone."

"Yes."

They walked off in different directions in search of the wetsuited kelp thieves.

Miller walked quickly, stopping to peek briefly into each store and business. The sun beat on the display windows, reflecting harshly and making his eyes smart.

"Should've worn my shades," he muttered. He pushed past meandering couples and groups, constantly scanning all around him.

Strange business for a scientist, he thought, scooting around like some private eye looking for evidence of an illicit liaison.

Seaweed eaters! Mark doesn't understand to what great lengths kids will go for a laugh around here. He should have shown Mark the clipping about those three beach boys a couple of years ago who went into a sweet shop, ordered a dozen huge sundaes, then took the ice cream, smeared it all over themselves, and raced out into the street dancing and singing and looking like three melting candles. They had done no real damage, and all that had been demanded was that they pay for the sundaes, which they did.

The only difference here, Miller supposed, was that the kids didn't pay for the kelp.

But that wasn't quite right, either. Mark wasn't so naive, and wasn't liable to go off half-cocked. If Mark thought it was possible these two had some connection with that spacecraft, it was worth checking out.

And if it turned out to be true! What luck the police had written it off. Because if there really was something to these two, it would be the most wonderful thing in the world, the most exciting situation, to have them come into F.O.R.'s hands first!

And so Miller continued searching diligently, door to door. He was about to look into Cap'n Curran's Fishing Wear, when he stopped short.

Ahead of him on the sidewalk, their backs to him, was a couple in wetsuits, one with long, blond hair. They were walking quickly away from him—suspiciously. He raced up to them, slipped past, then turned to confront them.

"Somethin' on your mind, buster?" said the one with long hair.

"Sellin' hot watches?" said the other.

"Uh, sorry, fellas," Miller croaked. "I thought you were somebody else."

"Well, we're not, are we, Pete?"

"Nope," Pete said. "Don and me never been nobody but ourselves."

Miller nodded, quickly retreated, and crossed the street, leaving the two wetsuited men laughing.

It occurred to Miller that in fact they could have been the pair who took the seaweed, if somebody mistook the long-haired one for a female.

But as he watched them walk off he decided that such a bull neck, barrel chest, and huge, hairy hands could never be mistaken as belonging to a female. That conclusion caused Miller even deeper embarrassment, since he himself had made the mistake.

He resumed his search, though with even less confidence and enthusiasm than he had when he began. His watch said he had only ten minutes more before he was supposed to meet Mark back at the car.

Mark could see the water of the canal sparkling in the sun at the end of the street, and he gradually advanced toward it, checking into every side street and alley on the way.

Being around this town, watching faces, cars, storefronts, and all movements carefully, reminded him of his first visit ever to an Earth town. It was over a year ago, but it seemed like an age. He had walked out of the Naval Undersea Center unescorted, and had gone into town—looking for what he wasn't sure. He recalled his nervousness, his confusion and curiosity on that earlier excursion, and wondered if the two he was searching for felt as he had then.

But one problem he had had then he also had now: he was running out of breathing time. He felt his joints begin to stiffen slightly, and his breath came shorter than before. He would need to get back in the water soon. Fortunately, by his reckoning, he would be meeting Miller in less than ten minutes, and they could drive directly to the F.O.R. lab where he could drop into his tank for a restorative, aquatic nap.

At that instant he heard a metallic crash. From down an alley ahead of him came the sounds of trash cans falling over and rolling around. And a shout. Several shouts.

He hurried around the corner and stopped to look down the alley. Two slender people in wetsuits, holding hands, were backing slowly past the trash cans they had apparently knocked over. They seemed to be backing away in terror from two small children who stood huddled together looking at them. One of the children had her thumb in her mouth.

A woman ran out of an adjacent yard and up to the children, quickly stooping to put her arms around them both. Other children came running to the scene.

The couple in wetsuits, fear widening their eyes, kept backing away, holding hands tightly, saying nothing. Suddenly they turned and fled down the alley and out of sight at the far end.

Mark trotted into the alley, up to the woman hugging the children. "What happened?" he asked her.

"Those two divers were walking through here, and my kids came out of our yard to talk to them, and they just kind of freaked out, like the kids had leprosy or something. I tell you, I get a bellyful of those weirdos from the beach around here. . . ."

Mark dashed to the end of the alley and looked left and right. He spotted them off to his right, headed in the direction of the seawater canal. They were walking fast.

Mark trotted after them. They began to run. The road doglegged to the left and then back to the right. They continued on the road. Mark darted down an alley that seemed to be a shortcut. He came out of the alley and headed back to his left. Through a corner store window, he glimpsed them approaching the intersection, walking more casually now, but repeatedly looking back over their shoulders.

Mark turned the corner and stood facing them.

They tensed, slowed, and then stopped, staring at Mark. They looked around. There was no one else in the area. At a distance of some five yards, they examined Mark from head to toe. Mark, in his swim trunks and jacket, stood still to allow them to inspect him all over. He looked them over just as carefully, though there was little to see, except their handsome faces and their wetsuits.

Long moments passed, during which only the eyes of the three made any movement.

Then slowly Mark raised his hands. He held them palms out, and spread his fingers, exposing the delicate webbing between them. They stared at the webbing, and at his eyes.

The woman began to raise her hands.

Just then a police loudspeaker broke the silence. "You two in the wetsuits. Just hold it where you are, please."

They spun toward the booming voice to see a prowl car easing down the street toward them.

"Just hold it right there!"

They backed toward Mark, then turned and quickly brushed past him.

"No, wait!" Mark tried to grab their arms. "It's all right! Please wait!" He jumped around in front of them, spreading his arms. They tried to push by. He moved back and forth in front of them, trying to corral them. "It's all right . . ."

Suddenly the two linked hands.

Mark lowered his voice. "It's all right. We are friends."

The man put his hand on Mark's shoulder.

Mark nodded. "We are—"

At that instant the woman put her hand on Mark's other shoulder, and the power of the voltage slammed Mark back against the wall of the building with tremendous force.

Mark sank slowly to the sidewalk, while the man and woman fled through the alleyway and disappeared among the backyards.

The police car squealed to a stop. One of the officers bolted after the pair. The other leaped to Mark's side. Another police car wailed around the corner and continued past the first, trying to follow the pair.

The officer kneeling beside Mark cradled his head and felt for pulse.

* * *

The couple tore through yards and around houses, until they eventually met the road again. They sailed down it toward the small footbridge that spanned the canal.

The second police car screeched around the corner behind them.

They ran up onto the bridge.

The car skidded to a stop, and officers piled out and ran after them.

Without hesitating, the couple leaped feet-first off the bridge and splashed into the water.

Two cops stayed at the foot of the bridge, two ran up on the span. They all scanned the surface for signs of the fleeing pair. They saw nothing but the gentle ripples that spread from their splash point in the water.

The canal was there mainly to provide links between the town's protected marina and the sea. It was not a long arm of water. The Pacific lay less than a quarter of a mile from the bridge.

The police officers looked up and down the canal, shading their eyes to see to the end where it emptied into the ocean.

That was the right direction. But from that distance they could not see the hands that appeared first at the surface. When the two heads ducked up, however, one sharp-eyed officer spotted them.

"There! At the end of the canal!" He pointed toward them.

The couple whose heads were above the surface looked back toward the bridge, watching the cops gesturing wildly in their direction.

They dropped back into the water, and their shadowy forms headed out into the sea.

Four cops now stood on the bridge, looking into the sun at the point on the ocean where the two heads had been. "I don't believe it!" said one. "They covered three hundred yards in thirty seconds!"

A second cop joined the one at Mark's side. "What do you think, Nick?"

"I don't know. Stay here. I'll call."

He jumped up, trotted back to his car, and slid in. He snatched the mike off the dashboard. "This is Eighteen-A-six. I need an ambulance at the corner of Second and Kind. Man down, barely breathing. Don't know if he's gonna make it . . ."

chapter 5

The medical examiner's report added little to what the assistant had told them, or to what Elizabeth already knew. The purple stain seemed not to be linked directly to the man's death. Still, there had to be some kind of relationship, for the stain was there when the divers were snatched over the side of the outboard, and now one of them turned up dead with the stain on his hand.

And apparently the stain had severe burning characteristics. If only the samples she had gotten hadn't deteriorated so quickly. By the time she'd been able to examine them, they seemed to be composed simply of inert, harmless, purplish particles.

But then a thought came to her: what if the divers had been in the water when that stain was issued around them? Surely it would have stunned and disabled—and perhaps even killed—them.

When the stain was in the water, she suddenly remembered, it was difficult to see through it. Perhaps it was basically a means of disguising the approach of the creatures who were attacking the divers. Maybe its qualities that caused burns on human skin were purely coincidental.

She thought of Mark and Miller in pursuit of the

seaweed robbers. Clearly, Mark thought these could be the creatures from the spacecraft. She knew there was turmoil within him, as he pursued them while believing himself to be one of their kind.

But if they were so prone to violence, how could Mark be like them? He was as gentle as any human she had ever known. She could not imagine him harming any living thing, unless it was for self-preservation. But the attack on the three divers had been aggressive and, as far as she knew, unprovoked.

She thanked the assistant medical examiner and was about to walk out the door, when she heard another police call come in. It was delivered as lightheartedly as the first.

". . . Forty-B-two here. We've just checked out that farmer who called in about his fence. Seems like his gate was damaged, just like he said, probably with an acetylene torch. And he seemed woozy, all right. But those two divers he said must have slugged him from behind his back—he's got no bumps or bruises on his head at all. We'll stay on the lookout for a man and woman in wetsuits. . . ."

She walked quickly to her car. If it was the same two, at least they didn't always kill. . . .

Miller was heading back to his car when he heard sirens and saw a police car careen around the corner of Second Street. He heard the siren wind down and then stop halfway down the block.

He was a few minutes late getting back. But Mark was still not there. He turned the car around and headed for where he had seen the prowl car disappear.

As he pulled up behind the prowl car, he immedi-

ately saw Mark lying on the sidewalk with a policeman bent over him. He sprang out of his car and
headed out, pulling off his jacket as he went.

"Hey you!" called another cop from within the
prowl car. "Where you goin'?"

Miller knelt down beside the policeman and
reached for Mark's hands.

"Hey!" said the cop, pushing him away.

"I'm a doctor," Miller said. He took Mark's hands,
laid them across his chest, and covered them with his
coat so the darkening webbed fingers wouldn't be
seen.

An ambulance siren wailed in the distance.

"We got a stretcher comin' for him," the cop said.

"My name is Dr. Simon. Here's my card. I'll take
him, officer. Would you help me put him in my car?"

"Doctor, I'm sorry, but we've already ordered the
ambulance. Be here in a minute. I can't turn him over
to you now."

"Officer, I know this man well. He works for me,
and he's in my constant care. He needs an injection,
which I can give him most quickly right back at my
office. You can check his I.D. with mine." He motioned to Mark's jacket pocket. "You'll see we have the
same address."

The officer reached into Mark's pocket and pulled
out a card similar to Miller's, and looked quickly at
both.

Mark stirred, and his eyelids fluttered.

"Look, officer, he's in trouble. I have everything he
needs. Just help me get him into my car."

"I don't know . . ."

"Please. Speed is essential." Miller slid his hands under Mark's side.

The cop scratched his head, then slid his hands under Mark's other side. The two carried him to Miller's car and carefully sat him up in the passenger seat.

"Thank you, officer," Miller said as he trotted around to the driver's side. "You've been terribly understanding and helpful."

The policeman nodded and scratched his head again.

Miller pulled away, and heaved a sigh of relief as he passed the ambulance which was just turning into the street. He reached for the car telephone and called the lab.

"Ginny? Elizabeth there? No, I don't need to speak to her. Just tell her Mark needs the tank right away."

Elizabeth met him at the driveway, and the two of them slung Mark's arms over their shoulders and lugged him into the lab. They put him on a collapsible stretcher and raised it as high as the top of the tank. They lifted him off by his hands and feet and lowered him into the tank. He sank to the bottom and lay there as if asleep.

"Okay," Elizabeth said, breathing heavily from the exertion, "what happened?"

"It's some kind of trauma. I don't know what caused it. At first I thought he had just collapsed from dehydration. There's no question that he was weakened from that, but that didn't knock him out. There was nobody else on the street, except the cops. I got him outta there a split second before the ambulance came."

"Whew!"

Mark began to recover, breathing more deeply. He stirred in the tank and rolled over slightly.

"His back!" Elizabeth cried. "What happened to his back?"

Blue bruises were spreading over his shoulder blades.

"One of the cops mentioned something about him being slammed into the wall there."

"Slammed? By what?"

Miller shrugged. "That's all I heard. There was no time to ask questions."

"Mark?" She leaned over the tank. "Can you hear me?"

Mark rolled back toward them, his eyes fluttering open. He nodded slowly. He sat up, wincing, as he slowly flexed his shoulders. For a few moments he sat blinking.

"Are you all right?" Elizabeth moved around to face him. "You okay?"

He rubbed his forehead and nodded. "I met them."

"Met them? Talked to them?"

He nodded again.

"What are they like?" Miller asked urgently. "Did they do this to you?"

"They did not mean . . . to do this."

"How could they not mean it?" Elizabeth said angrily. "Look at your back!"

He flexed his shoulders painfully. "I cannot look at my back. But I can feel my back. It was when the police came. They became frightened. They thought I meant harm to them. They felt surrounded. They were defending themselves." He looked away from her. "Elizabeth, they are my people. Tall. Erect. Graceful. Strong." He looked back at her, smiling now. "And like this." He held his palms up and spread his fingers. "They are my people."

"You said you spoke to them?"

"Yes."

"What did they say?"

"Nothing."

Miller wrinkled up his nose. "Nothing? Is this a riddle? Couldn't they talk?"

"I do not know. I spoke to them. I told them I was a friend. I told them to wait. But when the police came, they ran." He looked off into the distance again, and lowered his voice to a near whisper. "I will look until I find them."

Elizabeth and Miller exchanged a concerned look.

"You think that's wise, Mark, after what they did to you?" Miller asked.

"They did not mean it. I do not know if it is, as you say, wise. It is something I must do." He turned his head slowly to aim his green eyes at Miller. "If you were alone in a world, with beings who were not your kind, and some of your kind suddenly appeared and then ran from you, you too would look until you found them. It is like the magnet of feelings which holds beings of one kind together. It is not something I understand, but something I feel. I think you would feel the same."

Miller rubbed his hand over his chin. "The radio said two people dove into a canal and disappeared underwater."

"Then they've gone back to the sea." Mark tried to raise himself.

"Mark, not yet!" Elizabeth said. "You've been injured."

Again he tried to rise, grimaced with pain, and sank back.

Elizabeth picked up her stethoscope from the desktop and put it carefully to Mark's back, moving it gently from one spot to another.

"They have a force like electricity in them," Mark said. "It was that force that must have caused me to hit the wall with my back. I felt the initial force, then nothing. Until now."

She turned to Miller. "Then that's how they attack."

"That's how they defend themselves," Mark corrected her.

Miller nodded. "Maybe they're leaving now."

Mark squirmed around in the tank, turning to put his hands on the edge and look at the scientists. "I must find them! If I don't, I might never learn about myself. I must find out who I am!"

"Mark," Elizabeth said calmly, "you're not *really* sure that they're your people. They could be any kind of alien—"

"This design on my trunks was in that spacecraft! Why? Why do they have it? Have you ever seen it before, anywhere? Why do I have the same thing? My hands, why are they the same as theirs? Can there be any answer but the one I have stated—they are my people!"

"We'll find out," she said in a soothing voice, "when and if we can. But in the meantime I'm going to notify the government and let them take over. This is bigger than we are."

"Not yet!" Miller raised his voice and a hand. "Not yet! I want to meet them! Elizabeth, how can you take a chance on bringing the government into this? Bunch of boobs in Washington with no more sense and brains than a babushka! Someone there might want to blow them to bits! Let's go out there! Maybe we can stop them from leaving!"

Elizabeth looked at him, then back at Mark. She was torn between accepting the greatest scientific challenge she had ever encountered, and her duty as a citizen. It was not the first time this had happened. She had been similarly torn about Mark in the beginning, when others wanted to immediately turn him over to Washington. He could be dangerous, they had said. But she had wanted to find out about him herself first. And she had prevailed. And she had been right; it had turned out well. If she hadn't held her ground then, Mark wouldn't be here with them now. . . .

"All right," she said softly. "We'll go out. But not Mark. He can't go with that back."

"I can go in the submersible!"

"I'm sorry." She had never heard him so upset, so insistent, so voluble. "I'm your doctor. You must rest. That kind of damage to the nerves and muscles of your back could suddenly cause it to spasm, tighten up. It could paralyze you temporarily, like a cramp. Only rest can avoid that."

"She's right, Mark," Miller added.

He turned away from them.

"We'll keep in touch with you by radio. Okay?"

Mark nodded.

She picked up the phone and dialed a single digit. "Ginny? Alert Wes, please. We have to go out again, Miller and I."

She hung up and moved with Miller toward the elevator door. "Be in touch soon, Mark. Take it easy, now."

He turned to look at them. "How will you communicate with them?"

Elizabeth looked at Miller.

"Our hope," Miller said, "is that they will try to communicate with us."

They entered the elevator, rode down in silence, and hurried through the tunnel to the sub pen.

Wes was standing at the gangplank. "Short notice," he said, nodding to them and smiling.

"I know," Elizabeth said. "Sorry."

"No problem. We're ready. We've hardly had time to get un-ready. Where we headed?"

"Same place."

"Roger. Mark?"

"We don't need him this trip. And he's already put in a tough day."

"Gotcha."

"Let's move. We're in a hurry."

They boarded, and Wes took the submersible out and headed for the B Sierra Trench.

Mark climbed laboriously out of the tank, toweled himself dry, and went over to the broad picture window that looked out over the Pacific. He stood quietly, as if deep in thought. Then abruptly he left the window and went over to a large tank filled with tall seaweed. "Joe?" he called toward the radio room.

"Yeah, Mark?" Joe Foley answered.

"Could you help me with something, please?"

"Sure thing." Joe came from the radio room with a bouncy step, whistling a disco tune. "What's up?"

"Would you please put some kelp on my back for me?"

"Sure."

Mark turned his back to him and leaned over against the aquarium.

"Wow, what happened to you?" Joe reached into the tank and pulled out a handful of seaweed.

"I fell against some rocks, in the current."

"Man, I'll say." He lay the kelp across Mark's back. "How's that?"

"That feels good."

"I didn't know kelp was good for that."

"Kelp is good for many things."

"Yeah, wonder if you could smoke it. Listen, you think that feels good, feel this." Carefully avoiding the bruises, Joe used the edges of his hands to beat a light, rhythmic tattoo across Mark's shoulders, down his sides, and over his lower back. "Doesn't that feel fantastic? Thing with bruises is, your muscles tend to tighten up. This is the best thing in the world for relaxing muscles."

"Where did you learn to do that?"

"My old lady. She was a masseuse. Even went to school for it. My old man was a drummer in a band where I grew up, in Alabama. The rhythm he laid on those skins really got to me, from the earliest I can remember. And then I got into signaling—you know, Morse code. I was the fastest key operator in the Southeast by the time I was twelve. So put 'em all together—massage, rhythm, code. Dig this . . ."

He performed some fast, rhythmic dit-dahs with the edges of his hands as he hummed "Alabama Bound."

"That's 'Alabama Kelp,' Mark." He laughed. "Morse is music. Rhythm is music. Music is music. I love to do it with my hands. How you feel now?"

"I feel much better. Thank you, Joe."

"Finished with the kelp?"

"Yes. That is sufficient. Thank you."

"You bet." Joe removed the kelp from Mark's back

and leaned over the tank to replant each stalk in the sand.

Mark went to the elevator and pushed the button.

"Where you headed?"

"I must check something downstairs. In the sub."

The doors opened and Mark stepped in.

"Hey, Mark, you forgot your—" the doors closed "—jacket." Joe's extended hand held Mark's jacket out toward the closed elevator doors.

Mark emerged from the elevator and moved at a half-trot down the tunnel to the sub pen.

The sub was already gone. Mark stepped to the edge of the dock and dived in. He flashed out through the pen and boathouse and into the sea, angling downward. It had been some time since he had swum at this forward speed. He was going all out as he sailed out and down into the Pacific. His bruised back didn't hurt now. And although he had not spent enough time in the aquarium tank to recover completely from his dehydration, the rush of water passing through his respiratory system at this speed provided him with swift and total restoration. His energy and stamina were not limitless, but he was not as easily tired as a runner or even a human swimmer. He could maintain his speed underwater as easily and naturally as a porpoise. And now, his excitement drove him even faster.

On and on he swam, his course as fixed and true as if he were being reeled in on a line.

It was some time before he saw the shadowy outline of the sub far ahead, and some time more before he caught up with it.

For all his prowess, he had expended a good portion of his energy in this pursuit, and so for a while he tailed the submersible, whose speed was, for him, relaxed. He glided along a bit above and off the stern to starboard, avoiding the turbulence left by the slowly spinning twin propellers.

Elizabeth, Miller, and Wes were watching the instant readouts produced by the scanning equipment. Elizabeth turned to the second officer.

"Watch for two blips. You're going to have to keep a sharp eye out. They're small, and they might not have any metal on them."

"Roger, Doctor."

"What do you think are our chances, Wes, of finding two things of that size?"

Wes wrinkled up his nose and scratched the back of his neck. "In this briny? Gosh, I don't know. We can sure pick them up, all right, if they're in the area. But it's a mighty big ocean."

"The closer we get to the spacecraft," Miller said, "the more likely we are to be in the area where they are."

"If that's where they're headed," Elizabeth said.

"Where else?"

"Well, like Wes says, it's a mighty big ocean. They could be anywhere in it."

"You still thinking this might be just a figment of our imagination, Elizabeth?"

She smiled wanly. "No. No, you're right. They're likely to be in that area. I was just being pessimistic."

"That's the difference between us," Miller said, chuckling and taking her gently by the elbow. "To you, problems are problems. To me, they're just the preface to solutions. I always assume things will work out."

"I know, Miller. That's a very good attitude. I should learn some of that."

"Hang around with me long enough and you will. And if I hang around with you long enough, it'll keep me from going off the deep end sometimes. That's why we're a good team."

"Thank you. It's sure nice not to be alone in something like this."

"Tell that to Mark. He's sure feeling poorly about it lately."

"I can understand that. Can't you? I sure hope it works out for him."

"We'll *make* it work out for him, Elizabeth." He beamed a smile at her.

She nodded and went back to scanning the readouts.

"We're making good time," Wes said. "We should rendezvous with the target shortly."

The second officer snapped his fingers loudly. "I have something." He leaned close to the scanner. "I'm picking something up."

They moved over to join him at the screen.

"See that? Little tiny blip at about five o'clock."

"Just one?"

"That's all I'm getting. Off the starboard stern, about five hundred meters behind us. Closing in."

Miller and Elizabeth looked at each other.

"Blip approaching," the officer went on. "Elevation twenty degrees at four o'clock. Range, two hundred meters."

"Must be one of them," Miller said.

"How could it have gotten behind us?"

"Must have circled around."

"Blip just off the starboard stern. Range, twenty-five yards. Holding steady. The thing is just sitting there off our rear end."

"Let's see it," Wes commanded.

The officer twisted dials and pushed a series of buttons. "Punching up video two, Captain."

The monitor lit up and showed at first nothing but empty sea. Gradually it panned around to coincide with the sonar scanner, stopped, focused in, and presented a clear picture.

"It's Mark!" Elizabeth put a hand to her forehead. "He's followed us!"

"I'll be darned," Wes said, shaking his head.

"That explains why he gave in so easily, back in the lab," Miller said.

"But—" Elizabeth shook her head. "I was going to say, 'But why?' But of course we know why. Tell Bobby-K to give us UNDER in here, please. I want to talk to him."

"Roger, Doctor." Wes picked up a mike. "Bobby-K, punch up UNDER for us."

"You got it, Captain. UNDER system lit. Go ahead."

Elizabeth slid onto a stool before the UNDER mike. "Mark? Mark, this is Elizabeth. Do you copy?"

Mark didn't answer, but on the monitor they saw him react to the message, suddenly turning in the water.

"Mark, do you copy? Please answer me!"

"Yes, Elizabeth," came his filtered voice, "I hear you."

"Mark, you shouldn't have come. You know that. But at least come aboard the sub, please!"

He didn't answer.

"Mark, we're going to find them, if it's possible. You can be of more help to us—and yourself—aboard the sub. Please come aboard!"

"Not yet, Elizabeth. I'm sorry. But I can find them more easily than you."

"No, Mark. We've got all our scanners and sensors working. You shouldn't try it alone. Mark?"

His face closed in on the monitor. He nodded and waved, then shot forward out of the picture.

"Punch up video eight!" she barked.

Wes snatched the mike. "Video eight, Bobby-K!"

The screen lit up with a new picture, from a more forward camera. Mark was just disappearing out of that camera's view.

"What's our speed, Wes?"

"Eight knots, Doctor."

"Then we're going to lose all sight of him in about thirty seconds. Depth?"

He turned to the gauge. "One eight hundred meters."

"How far are we from the target?"

Wes looked over at the second officer.

"Sixty-five hundred meters, sir."

Elizabeth paced nervously back and forth. "We picking up Mark on anything at all?"

"He's still on the scope, Doctor," the second officer replied. "Just barely, though."

She put her hands to the sides of her head. Then she lowered them and clenched her fists. "Everyone alert! Be ready for anything, Wes!"

"Hey, Elizabeth," Miller said, smiling and putting a hand on her arm, "take it easy. You're going to drive everybody crazy."

"Miller, it's just that—it's just—darn it! We don't know what we're dealing with here!"

"We all know that. Wes knows that. This crew is always prepared for everything. That's the nature of this business."

"I know, I know, I know!" She stomped back and forth, her fists clenching and unclenching. "But this—the implications of this—could be terrifying!"

"Elizabeth." He blocked her path and took her shoulders in his hands and looked into her eyes. "I've been in the marine-science business for over ten years. And not once have I run into anything terrifying."

"But this, this is different, it's—"

"Hey, let's cool it, okay? We're all taking our jobs seriously. We're all okay, you know? We'll handle it better if we're cool."

She studied his face, then gradually relaxed and smiled thinly. "Okay."

"Good."

"But stay alert!"

"What do you say, Wes, should we stay alert?"

"Yup."

"Okay, Elizabeth, we're all going to stay alert."

They all shared a brief laugh, then quickly turned to the various scanners and monitors. For a while the sphere was silent.

"I've lost Mark on the scope."

Heads turned toward the second officer.

"He went off the edge. I lost him. Sorry."

"Not your fault, Jim," Elizabeth said grimly.

"All hands!" Wes barked into the mike. "Look lively now! Helmsman, steady as you go!"

*　*　*

Mark swam steadily down, not on a straight line, but in a smooth arc, looking right and left at the canyon walls. Finally he approached the bottom and hung jellyfish-like above it. He turned a lazy loop, examining the terrain in every direction.

He gently undulated forward, then stopped again and scanned the ocean floor.

In the distance, he saw it: the entry tube of the spacecraft.

He did not speed off toward it, but approached slowly, cautiously. It loomed ahead of him, starkly angular, silent, and isolated, reaching up from the sand like a rigid, metallic, predatory plant whose mouth lay open in wait for a passing squid.

At least he was atop it. He swam around it gracefully, effortlessly, surveying it for signs of life.

Seeing none, he dipped down and was about to enter it, when a slight vibration in the water caused him to spin around.

The two beings were approaching the tube from above him. They swam in undulatingly as he did.

Mark left the tube and swam a few yards toward them, stopped, hovered, and spread his arms to indicate friendship, and to show that he was unarmed.

They swam slowly and steadily closer, their eyes never leaving him.

Mark held his arms wide, but made no further advance.

As the distance between them narrowed, the two seemed to have no communication with each other. Their pace was calm and deliberate; nothing in their motions indicated hostility or fear. Had the circumstances been different, it might seem that they were approaching Mark with nothing more than simple curiosity.

When they were but a few meters away from Mark, they stopped. All three hung nearly motionless in the water. The two looked Mark up and down, as he did them. For some seconds there was nothing but this cool mutual examination and evaluation.

No police would arrive to interfere with this meeting. But Mark was apprehensive about the pending arrival of the sub, which might have the same effect. He moved a couple of meters closer to the pair, still holding his arms spread.

Now the male moved off from the female, circling to Mark's right side but keeping his distance. He looked back and forth from the tube to Mark, as if he might be distressed about Mark's proximity to the craft.

Mark turned to him, his arms extended. "I am a friend," he said.

The male looked at him, and back at the tube. He made no response of any kind.

"I am a friend."

The male looked back at the female. And as if that were a signal, she glided around to the opposite side of Mark.

Mark backpedaled a few feet, trying to keep them both in view. He saw the male clasp one hand on his other wrist, and saw the female nod. Mark shook his head. "No, no. I am a friend. I am here in peace."

They advanced on him from either side.

"No . . ."

They reached for him. He flipped upside down and dove for the tube.

He swept inside, then pressed himself against the wall.

Immediately the male entered the shaft, head down. Mark grabbed him, applied a deft headlock, and twisted sharply. The male went limp and tumbled slowly down into the spacecraft.

Mark followed him down, reached him, felt his pulse and chest, and assured himself that he was only stunned to sleep.

Then he leaped back up into the funnel.

The female was hovering nearby. Mark emerged and swam directly toward her.

She kicked sharply, looped downward, and tried to avoid him in an effort to reach the tube.

But Mark intercepted her by grabbing her arm. They twisted and turned and kicked wildly. She was strong, and panic made her stronger. But her thrashing was only defensive; she was not an attacker, but tried only to escape Mark's clutches.

She managed to free herself and darted away. But in their tussling she had become disoriented, and mistakenly headed not for the tube but in the opposite direction. In the moment it took her to recover her equilibrium, Mark was on her again, seizing her from behind, quickly slipping one arm around her neck and twisting sharply to tighten the pressure-grip. She went limp just as her companion had.

Her pulse was steady, her breathing normal.

"Elizabeth!" He strained to see through the sand-filled water, roiled by their thrashing. He shouted to be heard over a distance he could not assess. "Elizabeth!"

* * *

It took her a few seconds to respond. When she first heard his faint voice, she was stunned. Then she recovered, scrambled over to the UNDER mike, waited another second or two for Bobby-K to throw the transmission switch, then answered.

"Yes, Mark!"

"Elizabeth, come to the spacecraft! Home in on my voice! I will enter the air lock with both of them! Please have somebody ready to attend to them!"

"We'll be ready!" she shouted, though not really knowing what that meant. She turned from the mike. "Wes, you heard?"

"Right. Ahead full! Right two zero! At depth! Crew, we're about to receive visitors! On your toes!"

Elizabeth grabbed another mike. "Prepare main air lock and emergency first aid!"

There was a bustling throughout the ship as the crew responded. The helmsman corrected course slightly. Bobby-K pressed his earphones tight to his head to insure he could hear anything Mark might transmit. The second officer scanned his scope closely, waiting to pick up the blips as they homed in on Mark. The airlock controller moved to his gauges, levers, and dials, checking pressure and hydraulic systems.

The submersible surged forward. Elizabeth and Miller went into the second sphere to be on hand at the airlock. Wes went to the first sphere to oversee the controls and approach.

Though the wait was short, to the scientists it seemed interminable. No one knew what to expect. To Miller—and to Elizabeth as well, though she fought the notion—there was a small question about Mark's state of mind. He had met the odd couple, and dealt with them in some fashion they didn't know, and now he was coming back with them. Was he, as he insisted, one of them? Would he, then, be like them, perhaps violent?

Would the three of them, Miller dared to ask himself, try to take over the ship?

But Miller answered that question as soon as he had posed it to himself: Mark was bringing back to this submersible two of the greatest finds of all time! It was not a threatening situation, but a wondrous and exciting one!

And so they waited those few minutes it took for the sub to gain the area. The blip was picked up on the sonar, and then they were there. The engines stopped, reversed briefly until the sub's glide ceased, then stopped again.

Towing the unconscious female, Mark moved up to the airlock door and pushed the button. The door slid back, and he deposited her within, leaving again as the door slid closed.

He dove down into the funnel, found the floating male, and towed him back to the sub. He pushed the button, waited for the door to open, shoved the inert form in ahead of him, and entered the airlock himself.

"They're in," the air-lock man announced.

Elizabeth went to the porthole and looked in. She saw the two still forms, and an apparently hale Mark beside them. "Okay, Wes, everybody's aboard. Get us outta here."

"Roger. Helmsman, let's go home."

The airlock man turned to Elizabeth. "Want me to empty it?"

"Right. Let's see what we've got."

He pulled the levers, and the hiss of entering air and escaping water filled the room.

As the water level in the airlock dropped, the two prostrate forms began to revive. The female was the first to rouse, rolling over and looking up at Mark. Then she slid over to the side of the male and prodded him. He too lifted his head and began to move his legs.

For a while they just recovered calmly. The water sloshed lower and lower and then the two of them stood up. The water was at ankle level. They looked at Mark. But it was not a tame appraisal this time. Their eyes sparked.

Suddenly they leaped at him, grabbing for holds while reaching for each other's hands. Mark lunged between them, trying to keep them apart. All three went down in the air-filled chamber, a mass of flashing arms and legs. They rolled around, bumping into the walls. Mark struggled desperately to keep them from joining hands and completing their potent circuit.

Hearing the commotion, Elizabeth jumped to the porthole. "Get them out of there! They're trying to kill him!" She hit an alarm button, and the repeated Klaxon blasts brought crewmen rushing in from other spheres to help.

The airlock man sprang to the door and frantically spun the wheel. Two crewmen pulled it open.

Other crewmen lunged through the opening and seized one of the pair, which happened to be the female, and hauled her out kicking and flailing her arms. Two more dragged the male out.

"Keep them separated!" Mark yelled. "Don't let them touch!"

Several more crewmen raced back from the control pod and dove into the fray.

The strong couple fought them furiously. They flung off man after man as they struggled to reach each other. Mark tried to get between them again, but he tripped over a crewman and went sprawling across the deck. Miller reached this way and that, but arms and legs kept buffeting him and throwing him back. Wes dove on top of the writhing mass of bodies, but was rolled quickly off by a foot in his belly.

Finally the male managed to extend his fingers to touch those of the female. They locked hands. The first person they touched was an unfortunate mate who absorbed the shock through his chest and was knocked back against the bulkhead. He sagged to the floor unconscious.

For a second that action stunned everybody; the crack of electricity sent a shock wave through the room. Then two other valiant crewmen dove at them, and suffered a similar fate, slammed backward and knocked unconscious by the voltage generated by the contact of the two aliens.

The fight ceased abruptly. The two aliens stood surrounded by panting, sweating crewmen. They held hands tightly and stared at their antagonists. Mark stood in front of them, tensed but still.

Crewmen blocked the bulkheads fore and aft. There was only the sound of heavy breathing. All eyes were fixed unwaveringly on the couple. And the couple's eyes were blazing back.

Elizabeth pressed against the side of the airlock, her chest heaving. Miller stood near her, breathing just as hard. He worked his lips as if to speak, but no words came.

At last the couple moved. They turned slowly around, still locking hands, and took a few steps toward the bulkhead leading to the control pod.

The eyes of the two crewmen blocking it darted left and right, as if looking for instructions. They sought the eyes of their captain.

Wes was as silent as the rest.

Elizabeth's eyes moved to Mark. It was to him that they must now look for guidance. He caught her look and answered it: he shook his head.

Elizabeth tried to speak. Her throat was clogged. She forced the words out: "Don't fight them." She saw Wes take a step forward, his fists clenched white. "Wes, everyone else, don't fight them. I know how hard it is, Wes."

Wes stopped and glared at the couple, his cheeks twitching.

The pair stood before the crewmen blocking the way to the control pod, staring at them menacingly.

"Let them through," Wes growled.

The crewmen instantly parted.

The pair strode through the bulkhead, followed at a distance by Elizabeth, Wes, and the second officer.

Mark and Miller hung back. As soon as the aliens had left that sphere, Mark ducked back into the stern.

The two aliens looked around at the controls. The male turned smartly to face Elizabeth. "Turn your ship around."

She stepped back, momentarily dazed by the sound of the male's first words. His face, she noticed for the first time, was quite human, even to the eyes. She had expected the eyes to be green, like Mark's, but they were gray, like many people's. The very humanness of their appearance—for he was lean and nice-looking, and she was exceptionally pretty, with large brown eyes and high cheekbones—made eerily ironic the fact that they were not. She gulped. "Do what he says, Wes," she said hoarsely. "We have no choice, right now."

Wes bared his teeth in a snarl, but nodded. He rotated his finger toward the second officer, who quickly stepped to the helm and swung it around.

The ship started a slow 180-degree turn.

Miller now came into the control pod, his step almost jaunty. He was smiling slightly, which made Elizabeth cringe. He glanced around, taking in the tensely hostile attitudes of the crew and the aliens. "Now what?" he asked brightly. "We going to play standoff?"

Elizabeth stared at him in disbelief. Then her look hardened. "This is not a joke, Miller," she said softly, though with a mean bite. "It's a time for brains. We've got a little problem here—" she glanced at the couple, who were eying her closely, and apparently listening just as closely "—and only someone with a lot of brains is going to solve it."

"Quite right, Elizabeth. I couldn't agree with you more. But by your tone you reveal your unfortunate continuing pessimism. There are brains galore at large in the realm of our work!" He spread his arms grandly, a gesture that caused the alien pair to take a threatening step toward him.

"Miller!"

"Oops, sorry, Elizabeth. I didn't mean to startle anyone."

She stared in quizzical frustration at her associate,

unable to comprehend this inappropriately casual manner he brought to such a dangerous situation. It was not that he didn't often act and speak flippantly in the face of tough problems; he did. But she had never supposed she would see him virtually laughing when the entire crew of the sub had been brought to its knees. And when there was no assurance at all that they would be left alive; or even that the nation would escape severe harm. "Miller?"

He arched his eyebrows pleasantly.

She snorted angrily and looked away.

chapter 6

The big submersible continued its wide about-face. The engines hummed faintly below decks, transmitting their vibrations through the hull to the soles of all the feet planted on the deck of the control sphere.

Elizabeth's immediate fear was not so much of the aliens, but of her own crew. These were proud professionals, and though peaceful, they were, among other things, well trained in the arts of self-defense so necessary in dealing with the wiles of creatures of the sea. For these men, the arts were not the martial ones so popular on land, but the disciplines of strength, quickness, alertness to danger, and courage that allowed them to dive in risky places.

Among the reasons they had been selected for this crew were that each demonstrated a fine affection for this work and a fierce commitment to its purposes. But they were not sheep; another reason they had been chosen was their lively individualism. They took orders well, but they were encouraged to think for themselves, as in the case of Bobby-K and his radio adaptations.

The short of it was, Elizabeth was not at all certain how long these proud, loyal, and courageous individualists could be expected to acquiesce to a takeover, and possible destruction, of the ship that they loved, cared for, and protected as eagles do their aeries. She didn't know how long she could keep their defensive capabilities and wills in check. The tension in the control room was palpable; the vibrations under their feet could as well be from the buzzing of nerves in baths of adrenalin as from the mechanical whirring of the turbines.

The strange hand-linked couple stood to one side of the controls, keeping their eyes on both the semicircle of crew standing to their left, and the hunched figures of the pilots seated at the controls to their right.

"One-eight-oh turn completed, sir," the second officer mumbled.

Wes nodded slightly and kept his narrowed eyes on the pair who were pirating his ship.

"Return to where you found us," the male said, "to our craft."

Wes curled his lip and hissed softly through his teeth, then nodded to the second officer and navigator.

Throttled forward, the engines increased their hum. The submersible began pushing ahead through the sea, retracing the path it had so recently made in normal fashion, but now under the command of aliens.

Wes ground his teeth, scowling. He looked obliquely at Elizabeth. "Dr. Merrill," he said tautly, "we can't let them take control of this ship."

"Wes, we have to," she said, aware of the inadequacy of her words. "We have no other choice now. I'm not risking more lives. We've had three people injured already, and if we're not careful . . ." she glanced at the couple, "we could all go."

"My apologies, Doctor, but we could all go anyway. At least we have to try—"

"This is a submerged vessel," she said more stiffly, "not a streetcorner. This is not a matter of a fistfight. This is life and death. Under the circumstances, we have to play it their way."

They were both trying to keep their voices low and even.

"It's our ship."

"For now, we do it their way. That's my order."

"Roger," he said, smiling sardonically.

She felt no anger at his rebellious tone; rather, she felt a curious pride in the reassurance that his spirit was unquenchable, while underneath it all, his loyalty to her was firm.

Miller began to hum a light, breezy tune, then edged back toward the bulkhead and leaned to look through it.

Again the hand-locked couple advanced a step toward him.

"Miller!" Elizabeth hissed. "Nothing rash, if you please."

He straightened immediately and turned back, his eyes widely innocent. "Who, me? Elizabeth, I'm not rash. Don't mistake my optimism for daredeviltry. I am," he raised an index finger, "no more or less than a brilliant coward."

"Do not move!" the male ordered.

"I'm not moving. I'll be still as a scarecrow if you want. Immobile as the Sphinx. Stolid as Lot's wife, though not so salty. I will move neither finger nor—"

"Miller!" Elizabeth wrung her hands as if they were around his neck.

He sighed and looked at the ceiling, then cocked his

head, as if listening for something. Finally he said, crisply, over his shoulder, "Okay, Mark, come on in!"

Through the bulkhead stepped Mark, or at least the general configuration of Mark. For he was entirely covered by a scuba suit, from his neoprene rubber boots to his neoprene rubber hood. His hands were encased in neoprene rubber mitts. His face was concealed behind a neoprene-and-glass face mask.

He walked quickly through the control pod and stood confronting the two who had so cowed the crew. They crouched slightly, holding hands tightly, eyes unblinkingly fixed on him.

Mark threw himself on them. He grabbed the head of each under an arm as they whirled him around, jabbing at him with their free hands through which flowed the energy of a lightning bolt.

"Mark!" Elizabeth screamed, starting toward him.

Miller quickly seized her and held her back. "He can't be shocked!" he bellowed over the din of the wrestling. "He's safe as a Goodyear tire!"

No sparks flew from their hands as they grabbed, probed, prodded, and beat in vain on Mark's insulated body. The crew stared on in dumb, openmouthed fascination at the wildly hostile rumpus the three wet-suited creatures were engaged in.

Straining to the limits of his strength, Mark drew their heads farther and farther apart, until at last the dangerous connection of their hands was rent, and he hurled the male savagely against the control panel.

The instant the pair were separated, the anxious crew pounced, those in the control pod quickly joined by others who poured in through the bulkhead.

The pair was subdued easily and efficiently. So swiftly was the proper order of command restored, the antagonists trussed and held harmless by a dozen arms, that it took some moments for the fact to sink in.

Crewmen and scientists looked at each other in wonderment, then in relief. Smiles and sighs broke out all around.

"Thanks, Mark," Miller said calmly. Then he turned to Elizabeth, smiling warmly. "You see, Elizabeth, there are brains aplenty, even in this humble solitary noggin of mine. And given the time and the proper attitude, brains can work things out."

Suddenly stricken weak from the tension she had been under, Elizabeth could do nothing but smile and shake her head in admiration.

Mark stepped close to the former captors, now captives. "I am sorry. I did not want to hurt you."

The male's glower had vanished. He looked at Mark, with an expression that revealed neither rage nor awe nor even comprehension. His face said nothing.

"Okay," Elizabeth said at last, "let's get back on course. Let's go home."

"Yes, ma'am," the second officer said, without waiting for the traditional relaying of the command from his captain. A certain informality reigned after the fellowship of battle.

"Wes, get the man into the main airlock," Elizabeth said, "and get the injured crewmen into sick bay." That last had, of course, been an unnecessary remark to make to the captain whose first responsibility, so consistently demonstrated in the past, was the safety of the crew. "I mean, you know . . ."

"Right." He smiled. "I know. We'll shape it all up." He beckoned to the three men holding the male, and they followed him out of the control pod into the air-lock area.

"Jim," she said to the second officer, "as soon as Wes gets back, take her and put her in the emergency airlock aft."

"Roger."

Elizabeth noticed the long and strange looks exchanged between the female alien and Mark. Such looks, though they might contain mysteries, were no mystery to her. And she didn't particularly welcome them in this situation. "Mark, you might as well shed that rubber skin, don't you think? It must be hot."

He nodded. "I am warm. If you think it is safe for me to leave—"

"Everything's fine. Go ahead back. See you in a minute."

He glanced again at the female and left the pod.

Hissing came from the air lock, and the door clanged open and then, after a few moments, clanged shut.

Wes reappeared with the crewmen. "He's secure and peaceful, though I can't say he's tickled pink about it. And we got the men into sick bay. My guess is that they're going to be okay, except for the fact that they may be dazed into next week."

"Good news. I'll check on them in a minute. Okay, Jim, take her out."

The officer and crewmen took the female out and back to the emergency air lock. Elizabeth watched them leave, then sagged into a high swivel chair at the control board. She closed her eyes for a few seconds. "Wes, would you mind if I said 'whew?' "

"Would you mind if I joined you?"

They both said formal "whews."

She turned to Miller with a wry smile. "Dr. Miller?"

"Hmm?"

"You and your college education."

He gave her a humble wave of the hand.

"For a while I thought you'd lost your mind. You sounded like an addled Pollyanna."

"I freak out on problems."

"Yeah, but next time let me in on the little dramas you're cooking up."

"Oh, my dear Elizabeth, I wanted to surprise you!"

"That you did."

Mark entered the control pod, dressed in his trunks and jacket.

"Well, Mark, congratulations." Elizabeth saluted him. "You were marvelous, as usual."

"Thank you." He stared vacantly out the forward port.

"By the way, you look like maybe you were zapped—and I don't mean with electricity."

He snapped his head around. "It is not a joke."

"Sorry. I didn't mean to be flip."

The second officer returned. "She's secure in the aft lock."

"Good. Thanks, Jim. I guess the helm's yours. I'll leave you to your seat."

Elizabeth rose, bowed to the chair, and headed out. Miller and Mark followed, leaving the control crew to themselves.

She walked determinedly back to the communications booth. "Bobby-K, will you get C.W. for me, please?"

"Right." He reached for the ship-to-shore phone.

"Hold it, Bobby-K." Miller put his hand on the phone. "Why, Elizabeth?"

"I want an escort for this vessel."

"What?"

"And I want armed guards waiting on shore."

"Wait a minute—"

"And I want underwater rescue to go out and get that spaceship."

"Hold it, Elizabeth! No way!"

"Don't tell me no way, Miller. It has to be done."

"He's right!" Mark said. "You can't do it, Elizabeth!"

She narrowed her eyes and looked at both of them. "What do you mean, he's right?"

"You can't mix science and politics!" Miller asserted, raising his index finger high.

"Oh come on, this isn't politics, Miller! It's national security! Even international security! We can't afford any more mistakes! We almost lost the whole shebang a little while ago!"

"Just the vicissitudes of the venture, Elizabeth. We handled it well, we came out of it fine, all by ourselves. We're still scientists, you know. We have to just keep taking it step by step, without the intrusion of governmental bumblers and military hardheads."

"Come off it, Miller! Are we back to that again? Haven't we learned our lesson yet? Even after all this? We've been flat-out lucky, so far. But we still don't know what we've got, out in those airlocks."

"You're right, absolutely right! Listen, we don't know what we've got, not yet. And we've got to know before we let the government get involved. If we don't keep it from them, and we ruin the chance to establish a relationship with these people—and maybe with their planet—a good symbiotic relationship that could last for eternity—*that's* how we'll be making a mistake! *That's* how we'll be letting this whole country down! We are more sensitive to the situation than those Washington warts could ever be!"

"Miller." Her voice wearied with exasperation. "These two are hostile and powerful. Every contact they've had with people demonstrates that. They aren't here on a friendly mission, to develop, as you call it, a good symbiotic relationship. Everything we know about them tells us they are aggressive and nasty."

"But that's just it, that's the trouble! So far all we've done is fight them, resist them with our own hostile means. There must be a better way of handling this. We can find that way, if you'll just—"

"Washington has to be told! And that's that!" She nodded to Bobby-K, who reached again for the phone but was restrained by Mark this time.

"Not yet, Elizabeth, please. I want to talk to them."

"*Talk* to them! You've *tried* to talk to them, *twice*. I don't think they go in much for chitchat."

"Yes, talk to them. Quietly. They are not simple beings, just like you are not a simple being. They are complex, and have fears and misgivings. Perhaps it would not be possible for you to talk to them. But I can get through to them. Don't forget, they are like me." He held up his webbed hands. "You saw that."

"Yes, I saw that. I also saw that in terms of psychological characteristics, they are as unlike you as—"

"Give us a little time," Miller persisted, "to understand what this is all about, for heaven's sake! You turn them over to the military, and that'll be that. I mean, they just don't have the Simon-Merrill viewpoint, if you know what I mean."

"I know full well what you mean, and you're right, as far as that goes. But that's not the point any longer. We just can't be sure we can handle them!"

"We can!"

"Let me talk to them, Elizabeth."

"No, Mark. No, Miller. I just can't withhold this information.

"Not withhold, Elizabeth," Miller said more calmly, "just wait a little."

"Something has to be worked out." She put her hand to her temples.

"You have to stall them—that's what has to be worked out."

She sighed. "I'm tired. You're always trying to beat me down."

"Come, come, Elizabeth. Why do you have to see things in such fretful, antagonistic terms? Neither Mark nor I is trying to beat you down. We're trying to convince you. We are all in this together. It's not one of us against the other. It's a project we have in common. All Mark and I are arguing for is to keep it *our* project. It's the chance of a lifetime!"

She dropped her hands languidly to her sides. "Something has to be worked out," she said softly.

Miller and Mark watched her silently.

"Okay, I'll think of something." She clicked on a microphone. "Wes? Has the tape been running all this time?"

"Sure has. Still A-okay."

"Good. Now, for the next few minutes, while I take care of the men in sick bay, I want you, all of you, to start recording your observations and impressions. Everything. I want this documented as fully as possible."

"Roger. We'll get right to it."

The sub rose gradually toward the surface as it homed in on its pen. Several crew members were seated around a recorder taping their recollections of the dramatic events that occurred immediately after the two aliens boarded. Wes paced back and forth behind the helmsman, keeping an eye on course and depth, inserting random comments for the tape.

Elizabeth moved among the beds in sick bay, where the three shock-stunned crewmen lay, now conscious, but still groggy.

"How do you feel?" she asked one, checking his pulse.

"Weak."

"Any pain?"

"Just a little, in my chest. It feels like I got kicked by a mule."

"How many fingers am I holding up?"

"Three."

"Now?"

"Two."

"Add twenty and five and eight."

"Ouch!"

"Come on."

"Thirty-two. Unh, thirty-three."

"Okay." She turned around to look at each crewman. "You fellas are going to be just fine. But I want you to take it easy for a couple of days. No work on the sub at all. Shore duty. Vacation. I'm proud of you all. And listen, keep your fingers out of light sockets!"

She left, smiling at the groans that followed her.

She walked through the spheres toward the control pod, silently passing Miller, who was reading some documents. Entering the control pod, she stood behind the captain, watching the gauges over his shoulder. "You're right, Wes, the guys are fine. I told them to take a couple days off. They're gonna feel limp as dish rags for a while."

He nodded without taking his eyes off the dials. "All right, ease her in now. Eight feet. Six feet. Four feet. Surface. Blow all remaining ballast. Clear all tubes." Hydraulic wheezings signaled the ordered discharges. "Prepare to evacuate main and emergency air locks."

The crew bustled into position throughout the ship.

C.W. Crawford had been sitting in a white wicker rocker placed for his convenience on the dock in the pen. Under the mercury-vapor floodlights in the rock-enclosed confines of the pen, he looked like a misplaced bwana. He was trying to focus his attention on a newspaper, but was fidgety, and kept looking up in anticipation of the arrival of the sub.

A few yards away, near the rock wall, a welder worked on a sheet of steel, his torch crackling with a blue flame. Annoyed by the noise and flashes of the flame and sparks, Crawford glanced occasionally in his direction, but he dared not tell a welder not to weld just because he didn't want to be disturbed. Fortunately, after a time the welder doused his torch to examine his handiwork.

At last a Klaxon blared its throaty announcement of the sub's imminent arrival, and the dock crew scurried into place. The conning tower poked up from the water, and the ship nuzzled into the dock and swayed gently in its own wake as the crew made fast the lines around the cleats.

Crawford watched over the top of his paper as the conning-tower hatch opened, and the captain's head appeared. Wes saluted the dock commander, then ducked back in.

After a moment Elizabeth appeared, climbed out, and came quickly over the gangplank.

Crawford casually folded his newspaper and rose, smoothing the legs of his pinstripe trousers.

"C.W.," she said brightly, "let's you and me take a walk."

"Now you're talking." His face beamed.

She took his arm, gave it a friendly squeeze, and led him toward the tunnel. He held his head proudly high in view of the crew, until he had the mischance to catch his foot under a welding hose and stumble forward a few feet. Regaining his balance, he ruefully noticed the scratch left on the toe of his black Gucci loafer.

"Sorry," Elizabeth said, "my fault."

"Don't worry about it," he said magnanimously. "Let's see now, what were we saying?"

"I was saying let's take a walk. I want to talk to you."

"Yes, fine. I happen to have a few spare minutes . . ."

Miller watched from the conning tower until they were out of sight. Then he had Wes dismiss the dock crew. Only the welder remained, tucked into a niche in the wall with his mask pulled down over his face as he tried to rekindle his torch.

Miller signaled below to the sub's crew. He climbed out and waited by the gangplank while the crew brought up the two aliens. "All right, move them up and out of her, fast!"

Mark led them up. Crewmen held the pair's arms tightly behind them. They crossed the gangplank.

"Careful, don't bruise them!" Miller directed. "Keep them separated! Watch the edge of the pier there! Take it easy now!"

The crew pushed them onto the pier, where they paused. Mark was standing near the female. They locked eyes.

She said softly, "You are not the enemy."

"Come on, come on!" Miller ordered. "Keep them moving!"

The crew thrust them forward again, moving toward the tunnel. The female glanced back over her shoulder at Mark, who was staring after her.

Just as they reached the tunnel entrance, the welder succeeded in restarting his torch, which produced a loud snap and a long flame.

The sight of the flare was a complete shock to the aliens, and they recoiled in a crouch, staring wide-eyed at the flame. In panic they yanked partially free and tried to bolt for the water. But the crewmen, assisted by Mark, quickly reinstituted their holds and hauled them back.

"What in blazes?" Miller rasped. "Careful, careful! Okay, okay, keep them under control! No rough stuff! Firm but gentle!"

They all disappeared into the tunnel just as the welder's torch went out again. He threw off his mask in disgust. Then he looked around. "Where the devil'd everybody go?" he murmured.

Crawford and Elizabeth strolled around the grounds and along the cliff overlooking the sea. Their relaxed pace belied the intensity of her message and the energy it generated in Crawford. She painstakingly and selectively recounted the recent capture of the strange visitors, omitting a few of the more upsetting details she deemed not helpful to her cause.

She also explained that there was a *quid pro quo:* in exchange for him being brought in on the matter, given responsibilities and access and information, he would have to follow the restrictions she outlined. He would notify the White House of this situation, and the White House would be privy to their discoveries, but the two aliens would remain under the exclusive custody and supervision of F.O.R. He was to make that clear, and was to stand behind it.

". . . So that's the story, and that's as much as we know about them," she concluded.

He had barely been able to contain himself as the full weight and import of the tale became more and more clear to him. He had, during the later stages of her account, begun to fidget, bob his head, and even occasionally skip along the path. He was a man imbued with a new and heady cause, a new stature, and a new source of potential glory. He was, as she concluded her tale, nearly busting.

"You've done it!" he crowed, doing a fast little run-in-place and pumping his fists up and down. "I mean, there isn't anything they won't give us now. If I want ten million, I'll get ten million!" He pounded a fist into his palm. "Twenty million! The first people from outer space, and I've—er, we've got them! I'll name my price, and they'll cough it up! Funding outfits will be crawling all over themselves to buy in! NASA will want a piece! National Science Foundation! Smithsonian! Interior! Civil Aeronautics! Wait till I tell Washington!"

"Hold it, now!" Elizabeth folded her arms over her chest. "Stop reacting as if this were a get-rich-quick scheme or some kind of ransom matter. This is serious scientific business."

"I can be cool, I can be cool!" Gradually he calmed down. Obviously it took great effort; sinews and muscles crawled along his cheeks and chin and hands to override other sinews and muscles that were causing him to squirm and twitch with excitement. Finally, he stood relatively still. "I can be cool. You'll see. Cucumber. Ice cube. Yes, I can handle this with aplomb. That's my natural style. You've come to the right person."

"There *have* to be those conditions I set forth. Nobody other than—"

"Yes, yes, you told me. I've got it. That's the deal. I can handle it. I'll work it all out for you. Have no fear, C.W.'s here. I'll make it a tidy little package. Can I see them now? Hunh? Can I? What do they look like?" He smoothed his hair back over his ears, and patted his jacket.

"I'll show you."

He looked at the sky and wiggled his fists in front of his chest. "Who'd ever have thought I'd be the one to notify the President? Such a meeting, such an intelligence briefing, will surely be recorded in the history books! We'll have coffee in the Oval Office, perhaps a few pictures for the press first—telling them nothing, of course!"

Elizabeth closed her eyes and sighed. "Come on, let's go in. But just take it easy. Try not to make everybody jumpy."

"Right, right."

They entered the building and went up the corridor to Ginny's desk.

"Ginny," Elizabeth said, "we're going into the lab. No admittance to anyone under any conditions, without my express permission."

"Roger."

When the crewmen, with Miller and Mark and a first-aid man with a red cross on his white jacket, brought the wetsuited pair into the lab by the back door, the aliens were still struggling. But as they passed by one of the aquariums, they suddenly ceased their resistance and stopped to look at it.

It was the aquarium in which Miller had earlier placed the gift rock, the rock that had inexplicably turned into a gray, carrotlike plant.

Now it was once again in rock form.

Miller, moving on ahead, had not noticed their interest in it.

They were pushed forward again, and resumed straining against the arms that held them.

"This'll do the trick," Miller mumbled. He stepped over to a Bunsen burner, turned the choke up, and lit it. The flame shot high, a brilliant blue-yellow. Miller picked up the burner and held it out toward the pair as far as its fuel tube would extend.

They crouched back fearfully.

Miller nodded benignly and lowered the flame. The two became docile. "Fix her up," Miller said to the first-aid man.

That was the scene that greeted Elizabeth and Crawford when they entered the lab: a nearly inanimate tableau of crewmen holding the docile aliens; Miller standing calmly holding the flameless Bunsen burner; Mark off to the side, his eyes on the similar beings he had captured.

Crawford's eyes got wider and wider, then narrowed. "They look a bit like people," he whispered to Elizabeth.

She shook her head and motioned for him to sit down on a bench. He sat down slowly and stiffly as if hypnotized.

"Elizabeth, come over here," Miller said. He was standing next to the male. She came over. "Here." He took her hand and placed it on the male's arm.

She blinked. "It's not a wetsuit."

"Look closer."

She bent to examine the material. "My God! It's skin!"

Miller nodded. "Right. Skin. And not only is it some kind of skin, it's sensitive to heat, and it bleeds."

"Bleeds?"

"Come over here."

They went over to the female, who stood while the first-aid man knelt beside her, tending to a small cut above her ankle. To staunch the bleeding, he was applying pressure with a wad of gauze.

Elizabeth stooped beside the first-aid man and closely examined the small, seeping wound. "How'd she get this?"

"From the scuffle," the man said. "Nothing serious."

"Ever seen skin like that before, Miller?"

"Nope."

"What does it mean?"

"I'm not sure yet."

She stood up beside the female and quickly snapped off a tiny strand of her blond hair. She walked across the room and sat down in front of a microscope and put the hair on the glass. "Where are those hairs Mark brought from the spaceship?"

"In here someplace," Miller said, rummaging through a welter of papers on his desk. "Here." He handed her a plasticene envelope.

She took a hair from that and put it under the microscope beside the other.

Crawford watched all this with the awe of a child at a magic act, leaning forward stiffly, his hands on his knees.

Mark came over to the female. He pointed to the emblem on his trunks. "Look at this," he said softly. She looked down at the design. "When we were in the water, did you see this marking?"

She looked at it for a moment, seemed to be studying it thoughtfully. Then she looked up at him with slightly narrowed eyes, but said nothing.

"This emblem is also in your spacecraft. I found it, on the broken piece of material. It is the same. It indicates that, in some manner, we are related. We are connected by this symbol. Then why did you want to harm me?"

Her eyes seemed to trace the features of his face, then focused on his eyes. Finally she looked away.

"They're identical," Elizabeth announced, still peering into the microscope. "What Mark found is the same."

"Which means?" Miller came over.

"I don't know. Not a heck of a lot, I guess. But it certainly establishes that it's their spacecraft—and we need to pull together every bit of evidence we have on everything, as if we were preparing a legal case. And I guess it means she must have been in the transparent box Mark described, at some time for some reason or other. All right, let's get to work." She leaned away from the scope and swiveled the chair around to face the room. "I want EKG's, EEG's, temps, saliva, blood tests, cuticle scrapings—the works." She rose and went over to a long table where she began to arrange her examination and analysis equipment.

The female's eyes followed her nervously, remained on her as she prepared her instruments for the tests.

"Are you here because of me?" Mark went on in a low voice. "If so, please tell me. I am not sure . . . who I am. Or where I came from. I have no memory of anything before they found me at the edge of the ocean."

Still she made no reply. She watched Elizabeth.

"I am sorry about your cut," he went on. "I did not mean for you to be hurt. I only want to understand you, and why you are here. Then perhaps I can help you understand these people."

No response.

Miller stood beside Elizabeth, watching her assemble her gauges and tubes. "If it's their natural skin," he mused, half to her, half to himself, "why does it look exactly like a wetsuit? I could understand it if it looked more like snake or alligator or salamander or toad. But why just like an ordinary neoprene diving suit?" He scratched the back of his head. "Maybe it's not their natural skin. Hmm? Maybe it's been manufactured somehow. Maybe they bought it in some celestial shop, or had it made to order by some firmamental tailor. Hmm."

He turned and walked over to the couple. "Is this," he pointed to their abdomens, "your natural skin? Is this what you were born in?" He waited for an answer, looking from one face to the other. Then he stepped over to a wall hanger and plucked off one of Elizabeth's scuba jackets and held it out to them. "Why does your skin look like this? Hunh? It's an uncanny replica, but it's not really the same. Why does it look the same as this? Don't you know?"

He sighed, hung up the jacket, and went back to Elizabeth. "Like talking to a set of clams. I'll agree with you, they can try a body's patience in some ways. What do you think?"

"About what?"

"About their skin."

"I think I'm about to wire them up and take some readouts and maybe get some answers to some of our questions. Perhaps including that one."

"Oh."

"Did you expect them to tell you their life story in a private interview or something?"

"No, nope."

"We're scientists, remember, not journalists."

"I know."

"You wouldn't ask your sea robin over there to explain to you how come he can both walk and swim, would you?"

"Nope. But these are like people. They can talk. They—"

"They're not tourists from Toledo, you know. They may be as different from us as that sea robin."

"Enough! You've impaled me!" He clasped his hands together and looked imploringly at the ceiling. "Pinion me not upon your cross of rhetoric! I am beaten and downhearted!"

"Help me set up these circuits, will you?"

"Sure."

They laid out the wires and sensors and tubes they would need to test the lean couple in wetsuit skin.

The only thing that saved Elizabeth's sanity in the face of Miller's playful flights was her firm knowledge that when there was work to be done, nobody turned to it with more efficiency and sobriety than Miller Simon. One of his tricks—which she had not fallen for recently—was to lure her into an exchange of jibes and jokes, whereupon he would suddenly shift gears and demand that she get down to business. He abruptly began to play the dour and diligent physicist while she was trapped in the silly mood he had projected just before.

In this case, she knew exactly what he was doing. He was as nervous and concerned about all this as she; it was his way of keeping their feet on the ground without lapsing into all-out fright and dismay over the awesome responsibility they had taken upon themselves.

"That's the wrong line you've plugged into the monitor there," he said.

"Oh, sorry." She replaced it with the right one.

Mark, meanwhile, having retreated while Miller asked the aliens questions about their skin, now stepped back to the side of the female. "Where did you come from?" His voice was a near-whisper. "How long have you been traveling?" After each question he paused a moment in case a reply should come. "Your craft functions under water. You have come from a water planet. I believe you came in a craft that was always filled with water."

No answer. No tic or flick of an eyelid communicated a denial or acknowledgment.

"Is that not so?"

Still nothing.

He looked about the room, his fingers pensively over his lips. Then he turned back to her. "Are you hungry, or thirsty?" He pantomimed eating, plucking imaginary food with his fingers, dropping it into his mouth, and chewing.

She looked at him, but said nothing.

He reached into the seaweed tank and plucked a few strands of kelp and offered them to her.

She looked down at the kelp for a few seconds, then glanced over at her partner. His unblinking eyes met hers. She looked away from Mark, heaving a barely perceptible sigh.

chapter 7

A Navy staff sedan, driven by a sailor, pulled into the F.O.R. parking lot and cruised up to the front door, where C. W. Crawford stood waiting nervously, shifting his weight from one foot to the other.

The passenger, emerging from the backseat before the driver could scurry around to open the door for him, was Grant Stockwood. Shorter than Crawford and a bit pudgy, he had a warm, round face and sleepy eyes, and wore a slightly rumpled brown suit. But his quick and forthright manner established him immediately, always, as a man to be reckoned with.

His position in Washington was not one that generated much publicity, or welcomed it. He was as unobtrusive as he was essential and influential—his importance was shown by the weight he pulled in decisions about which the public knew almost nothing but felt in large and small ways on a daily basis. His title— even that not generally acknowledged—was Special Assistant to the President for Security Affairs. When he was introduced at the White House, it was usually as a personal aide.

Crawford came quickly down the steps, his hand extended all the way, until he bumped it into the handle of Stockwood's attaché case. Crawford pulled his hand back, stuck it out again, and finally shook the hand of the man from Washington. "Mr. Stockwood, I'm honored you came all that way so quickly."

"Mr. Crawford." He nodded perfunctorily.

"Call me C.W. everybody does." Crawford stepped back, composed himself, and spoke in a manner as businesslike as he could muster. "Mr. Stockwood, before we go inside, there are some things I have to say. This is a big moment. I think I am bound to give you a brief preface before we actually go in."

"Okay, let's hear it," Stockwood said briskly, fidgeting with his briefcase.

"Well, um, unh, you see, unh, it's this way. About our necessary ground rules. Um, well, we unh, here at the Foundation, unh, in order to protect our, um, interests—and of course those of the nation—unh, we feel that we must insist that the information about this, um, be restricted to—"

"You told me that over the phone."

"Yes, of course. And also that little bit about control . . ."

The male and female aliens had been put into large tanks like the one Mark used, and they were now wired with sensors attached to various parts of their bodies. Both Elizabeth and Miller had been surprised that the pair had offered no resistance at all to this procedure, but they were alert for any sudden change. Mark stood nearby. A few crewmen lined the walls for security.

The two scientists worked quickly. They stood at the table checking readouts from electrodes mounted on the pair's chests and foreheads.

"Wow," Elizabeth said softly. "He's got thirty-five

hundred volts negative. She's got almost four thousand positive!"

"If that's how they kill or stun," Miller said, "what happens to *them* in the water?"

"Maybe they can't complete a circuit in water."

"They'd have to. How else would they reproduce?"

As Elizabeth pondered that, Miller answered lightly: "Shockingly, that's how."

Elizabeth winced.

Mark kept his eyes on the two in the tanks; their gaze was fixed steadily on the scientists, whose conversation they seemed to follow with interest.

Elizabeth said, "What could there be in those two to produce such massive electricity?" She waited to hear Miller's joke about "batteries" or "transistors" or "a thick shag carpet."

"I don't know," Miller said. "But we'll have to find out before we can really deal with them."

The rear door opened, and Crawford quietly brought Stockwood in. They stood off to the side, watching.

Then Elizabeth and Miller turned to them.

"Dr. Merrill, Dr. Simon, this is Grant Stockwood," Crawford said proudly, "the special representative of the President."

Stockwood stepped forward and extended his hand to Elizabeth. "You're Dr. Simon?"

"I'm Elizabeth Merrill. This is Miller Simon, the director."

"Hi," Miller said, taking his hand in turn.

"And Mark Harris," Elizabeth said, beckoning him over. "I'm sure you know about him."

Stockwood shook hands with Mark.

"And over here we have the male and female from

places unknown. You two, this is Grant Stockwood, from our government."

Stockwood stepped over to the tanks. "Welcome to our planet," he said evenly.

The male glanced at the female, then reached his hand out over the top of the tank to her. He stuck his other hand out to Stockwood. Before anybody could react, Stockwood had taken the male's hand in his left, and was about to take the female's proferred hand in his right.

"Don't shake hands with them!" Miller leaped to pull Stockwood's hands away. "They can kill you!"

Stockwood stepped back, confused. "But I thought they were offering to—"

"When they're touching each other they're the hottest storage battery you ever saw! When they touch you, they're completing the circuit. Whew!"

"Sorry."

Elizabeth, first relieved that Miller had acted quickly enough, now saw that Stockwood's expression had changed.

He stared at the couple in the tanks for a moment, then turned to Elizabeth with a grim look. "Dr. Merrill, obviously you're dealing with something extremely dangerous here. That could be a problem."

"What kind of problem?"

"Well—"

"Mr. Stockwood," Crawford put in, "you agreed to let us continue with our work for a while without strictures."

"I know what I agreed to," he said stiffly.

Crawford looked at the floor.

"Sir," Mark came forward, "did you notice their hands?"

"I did."

"They're like mine." He held his up.

"I see. Are you also charged?"

"No. I do not believe so."

"Well, these two are, apparently. In dealing with you all here, I must take into account any threatening circumstances. Mr. Crawford unfortunately did not advise me of this particular aspect."

Crawford flushed and shifted his feet.

"Sir," Mark went on, "it isn't only Dr. Merrill and Dr. Simon who need time. I do. To be able to communicate with them."

"You?"

"Yes, sir. We are much alike in many ways. I believe I can communicate with them meaningfully. I believe they will talk to me, if I am given time to approach them in the proper way."

"I see." Stockwood cocked his head and rubbed his chin. "Of course, it goes without saying that such communication would be valuable. But it is the question of the intervening time that disturbs me. If there were, say, an accident, and somebody got hurt. Or if they were to get free . . ."

For a few moments Crawford seemed to be inwardly wrestling with something. His eyes had snapped wide, then narrowed, then rolled around. A couple of times he had opened his mouth to speak, but had said nothing. Now he spoke, hesitantly. "Everybody's going to think I'm, unh, weird maybe. But I've seen these people somewhere before."

All eyes, including those of the couple in the tanks, turned toward him. He shuffled his feet and shrugged his shoulders. Elizabeth glanced at Miller, then at Stockwood.

When no elaboration was forthcoming from Crawford, Stockwood smiled drily. "Why don't you scientists go back to your work. For the moment, I'm here only to observe."

They returned to their readouts.

Crawford's nose wriggled like a rabbit's, as if he were sniffing out something promising. Suddenly he went over to the bench where he had been sitting and picked up his newspaper and opened it to page three. "Here!"

Heads turned toward him again.

"Look here! They're right here! Here's their pictures! That's where I saw them!"

They gathered around him to look at the page. Under a headline,

WITNESS CLAIMS THREE MISSING
DIVERS WERE PULLED FROM BOAT

were three one-column head shots. Under the first two, labeled "Still Missing," were the names of Dilly Brice and Charles "Chazz" Jameson. Slugged "Found Dead" was the photo of Herbert Wayman.

"See?" Crawford said. "It's *them!*" He waggled a finger toward the tanks.

The faces of the pair in the tanks were unmistakably the same as the faces in the newspaper.

Elizabeth anticipated Stockwood's questions. "But these two are definitely not those human divers, Mr. Stockwood. It's all documented, right here. We've got two dozen witnesses to their special powers and constitutions. And you yourself can see, right now, right on these gauges, what's being generated in those tanks."

Listening carefully to her words, he nodded slowly. He was watching the pair in the tanks, whose passive expressions seemed to deny the revelations about them.

"Dr. Merrill," he said after a time, "does this mean what I think it could mean?"

"It depends on what you think it means."

He paused. "Suppose for the moment we accept all your evidence and documentation as being irrefutable. Could it mean that these people—these beings—are in someone else's bodies?"

Crawford's discovery had come so suddenly, with such eerie implications, that Elizabeth needed some time to compose herself before answering. She wanted her response to be as coolly scientific—or at least as cogent—as possible. "That's not something we could know for sure, just now, Mr. Stockwood. But that possibility definitely must be considered now."

"Then we're talking about murder."

Stockwood's sentence hung in the air.

Mark glanced quickly at the pair.

Elizabeth rubbed her eyes.

Finally Miller cleared his throat to speak. "Mr. Stockwood, if these people's bodies are right here, it's going to be pretty hard to establish a case of murder. No *corpus delecti*, if you know what I mean."

"No sophistry, if you please, Dr. Simon."

"Not at all, sir. I meant it not only as a legal point, but as a practical one. It's more a case for science."

"We don't know if they inhabited them," Elizabeth put in quickly, "or duplicated them."

"This is all so weird," Stockwood muttered. Then he said, more firmly, "If they have a way of taking over people's bodies, or a device that can duplicate them, we have to see it. We have to *have* it. I'm speaking with unabashed simplicity now, but that's the bottom line. If they have that capability, either way, we have to control it. There can't be any other consideration. We're talking about national security, and that's the bottom line for everything." He looked around at each nervous face. "I'm sorry, but I'm going to have to take charge of them."

Miller glanced at Elizabeth, who glared at Crawford, who looked at Stockwood with woeful, pleading eyes.

"But sir," Crawford said in a quavering voice, his arms outstretched with palms up, "we had the government's word on this."

"You had *my* word. But the situation you described was not exactly what we're dealing with—not anymore. With what's developed here, I can't stay on the sidelines any longer."

"Maybe if we called the President—"

"Dr. Simon, I can assure you, if you called the President, the call would be referred to me. Or if it wasn't, if you talked to the President, he would ask me to determine a course of action. I'm not bragging, Doctor, I'm saving time."

"Sir," Mark said softly, "is it not possible that by saving time you will lose something much more valuable—the chance to communicate with them?"

"Possible, Mr. Harris. But possibilities are not as important to me as likelihoods. Unlike science, where you sift all likelihoods and possibilities until you finally arrive at a truth, government cannot ponder all matters until the final truth surfaces. To avoid disasters and calamities, we must act on the basis of likeli-

hoods. There are suggestions of very ominous likelihoods with these two beings here."

"Sorry I remembered the newspaper, Dr. Merrill,"
Crawford said lamely.

"I'm going to call the Navy," Stockwood went on. "I
want their spaceship raised and examined, and a full
examination of them too. I'm going to have them
locked up until I can have them transshipped to
Bethesda."

"If you lock them up, sir," Mark persisted, "they
may never talk to you."

"That's a risk I have to take. It's less than the other
risks if I didn't lock them up. We'll try to debrief them
thoroughly over several weeks. Mr. Harris, you can
visit them after we're finished with that."

"Mr. Stockwood," Miller said, "if you did that to
me, I wouldn't tell you about the wonders of my
world."

"I'm not sure I care about—"

"But we will tell it." Stunned faces turned toward
the male, who had stood up his tank. "Yes. I will tell
you. We have such a machine."

He looked at the female, and she rose too.

Crewmen tensed alertly along the wall, but Elizabeth held up her hand to stay them, never taking her
eyes off the two beings in the tanks.

"It is time," the male went on, with no threat in his
voice. "I am named Xos. She is Lioa." He looked at
Stockwood. "We will go with you. We will tell you everything."

Lioa spoke. "It will be as Xos has said. And to you,
Mark, we will also speak." She smiled into his glazed
eyes. "Yes, we know of you. Especially I know of
you."

"We will go with you," Xos said. "We will cause you no trouble."

The two climbed down from the tanks. Elizabeth nodded to the crewmen and they came forward to surround the pair, but made no attempt to seize them.

Stockwood stepped through the ring around the aliens, eying them carefully. "I sincerely hope you're telling the truth," he said, icily.

Xos made no response, but offered his own wintry look.

"Let's go," Stockwood said.

They all moved toward the door.

Then Lioa turned to Mark. "It would be best if we could stay here and talk to you. But there seems to be no other way."

Mark clenched his fists. "There is a better way! Elizabeth! Stop him from taking them! Let us keep them here. Guarded, if necessary, but here!"

"I'm afraid I can't stop him, Mark." Elizabeth seemed near tears, but no more so than Miller. "He's got the whole weight of our government behind him."

"She's right, Mark," Stockwood said, firmly but not harshly. "It's done. I'm sorry. May I use this phone?"

Elizabeth pushed it across the desk to him, nodding glumly.

The scene in the parking lot astonished and appalled the scientists. It was full of Marine MP's, standing by two vans parked nearly back to back. The rear sections of the vans were windowless; the rear doors stood open. A lieutenant saluted.

Elizabeth turned angrily to Stockwood. "What's all this?"

"I told the vans to follow me by twenty minutes, so

it wouldn't spook you, Dr. Merrill. I didn't know what to expect. I had to make sure I was prepared."

Several MP's came forward and led the couple to the vans.

"Your promise didn't mean anything!" Elizabeth spat.

"I hoped you'd understand," he said, for the first time seeming slightly defensive.

"Oh, I understand, all right!" She glared out at the Marines, her former allies in the Navy, who were hustling Xos and Lioa into separate vans.

The lieutenant checked the closed doors, then called, "They're inside and secure, Mr. Stockwood."

"Then let's roll." He looked for a moment at Elizabeth, then lowered his eyes and walked off to his car. The car led the caravan out.

Mark stared after the vans, clenching and unclenching his fists.

Elizabeth went over and put a hand on his arm.

He sloughed it off, without meeting her eyes. "You are not helping me."

"I tried, Mark. Sometimes I have problems. And I need help too. You know how much I wanted to keep them here."

"I was wrong to take them captive."

"You did what had to be done."

"For the government, and for you. But not for me. And not for Lioa and Xos."

"Mark, I have never felt this anger from you before."

"You have not before given me cause for anger."

She put her hands on her cheeks. "Mark, don't treat me this way. We must trust each other. That is the bond between us. Don't destroy that, I beg you."

His voice turned even harsher, like a growl. "It is not I who destroys."

"Nor I!"

He turned to face her. "I want to be with them."

"You can't, now."

"We will see."

Abruptly he turned on his heel and walked away toward the corner of the building.

"Mark, where are you going?"

"Do not follow me, Elizabeth!"

She had started after him, but now stopped in her tracks. Mark disappeared around the corner. She became aware of Miller standing just behind her.

He put a hand on her shoulder. "Elizabeth—"

"No, don't talk just now. I'm going inside."

She stood on the widow's walk that surrounded the thick, round lighthouse tower. Hands clasped at her waist, she stared out over the cliffs toward the sea. It was a place and a view that had always given her deep satisfaction; it was from here that she surveyed the domain of the Foundation when she first arrived; it was a view that encompassed her plans and dreams, her future. It was a place she came for solitude, to think and reflect on her work and life, which, inseparable as they were, gave her great pleasure.

But now she stood with neither satisfaction nor pleasure. Her shoulders slumped a bit, her eyes sparkled not with beauty and dreams and the reflection of the broad Pacific, but with simple tears.

Miller came out quietly and stood beside her, looking off in the same direction.

In the distance below and beyond the cliffs, Mark was walking along the sand toward the surf. He threw off his jacket and plunged into the waves and vanished.

Elizabeth took a deep, choked breath. Miller put his arm around her.

"Miller, I've lost him. I think I've lost him."

chapter 8

Far out into the Pacific Mark swam; as aimless as the giant swells that roared up and rolled in, charting no course until they gained a landfall and then gathering all their might only to self-destruct against the shore.

Hours were not something that concerned Mark any more than they did the ocean. He glided around the depths for a long time.

But he was not mindless like those rocking blue waters tugged by the moon. And the thoughts that filled his head sloshed around like a stormy, confined sea, clashing, mixing, then separating anew.

For he was a creature of the sea now beckoned by the land. His feelings were strong and confusing. He was bemused by the currents of emotion that pulled at him. In time, drawn by the tides that pulled him from within or without, he surfaced to see the shore. It was not the same shore he had left some hours ago, but it was a shore, and the sight of it sealed his resolve.

It was a shore he wanted. Not the one he had just left; not the one where he now stood; but one not far from where he was.

❈   ❈   ❈

Miller strode through the front door and stopped at Ginny's desk. He cradled a package in his left arm.

Ginny was on the phone. "Vorremmo vederLa, professore. Si, dottore Merrill e dottore Simon, tutti e due saranno qui nel mese de giugno. Va bene, li diro."

She hung up and looked at Miller, who had raised his eyebrows expectantly. "Professor Salmaggio from Capri wants to know if he can see you both when he comes over in June."

Miller nodded toward the lab. "How is she?"

"Miserable, I'm afraid."

Miller pursed his lips, nodded, and went into the lab.

Elizabeth was gazing forlornly out the picture window at the ocean.

"Hi, my dear Elizabeth."

She turned. "Hi."

"You're taking it pretty hard, I must say."

"He's the only water-breathing Mark Harris there is." She tried a smile.

"I brought you something."

He handed her the package, and she sat down at the desk and opened it. She laughed when she saw it contained a plastic mechanical fish. She wound it up and dropped it into a tank. The little fish wobbled through the water, banging its nose against the glass; turned, banging its nose into the opposite side; turned again, and wobbled down the length of the tank.

"I love it! Thank you!" She touched Miller's cheek.

"I'm glad. Elizabeth?"

"Hmm?" She was watching the fish.

"Would you feel better if we went looking for him?"

She sighed and leaned back in her chair. "If he wants to hide, we won't be able to find him. Plus, if he wants to hide, there's no point in finding him." She pulled a microscope closer to her and focused in on the slide. "Boy, I sure don't feel like working."

"What have you got?"

"I think you could say, Dr. Simon, that I'm actually staring idly down a tube looking at some magnified dust." She looked up and chuckled. "Actually, *actually* I'm looking at some samples of the water from the tanks where Xos and Lioa were. Trying to see if anything washed off."

"And?"

"Nothing. They're clean as whistles. Today is one of those days when I wish I were a regular family doctor with a regular practice. You know what I'd do?"

"What?"

"Play golf."

They shared a laugh, which waned quickly into silence.

She turned again to stare out the window. "I wish he hadn't been so angry when he left."

The lights on shore were familiar to Mark; they were the lights of the Navy Yard. He ducked under the water and swam rapidly to the northern terminus of the lights. When he surfaced again, he was in the ship channel.

He saw several ships outlined against the shore installations, but they were not what he was looking for.

A propeller churned closer and closer to him, and he slipped under and swam away.

He wound through the channels and along the quays, surfacing for an occasional quick scan. Then he swam back out, surfaced, and surveyed the entire installation.

Moored not far offshore was a barge marked: U.S. NAVY SALVAGE. Two uniformed guards patrolled the deck, walking their tours in opposite directions. They carried rifles Mark knew were powerful enough to penetrate deep into the water.

Mark eased closer, his gentle undulations making no sound, nor leaving any wake.

At the foot of the wharf which jutted out toward the barge two vans were parked. He recognized them as the ones that had borne Xos and Lioa from the Foundation. A fence which extended out into the water protected the barge from trespassers.

For a while he gazed at this scene, watching the guards march to and fro, hearing their footfalls across the water.

He dropped under the water and moved closer. Now just a few yards off the bow of the barge, he surfaced silently. He slapped the water lightly with his hands, then ducked under.

One of the guards stopped and looked into the water, seeing a ripple but nothing else. He resumed his methodical pacing.

Mark repeated the slap.

The guards converged. "You never see them jump like that during the day, when maybe I could slip out here with a rod and line."

"Everything jumps at night, kid," said the other.

Mark surfaced again, and this time emitted some sharp squeaks.

"Hey," said the younger guard, "that sounds like a dolphin."

"Yeah. It does."

The two walked over to the bow rail and looked

down into the water. They waited for their dolphin to reappear.

While they stared into the inky water, Mark circled and then climbed soundlessly onto the far side of the barge. In one hand he carried a small, smooth stone. He lofted the stone carefully out over their heads. It splashed into the water in front of them.

"He's coming closer," the older guard whispered.

"Maybe he wants us to pet him. Maybe he escaped from some aquarium and wants one of us weird things called human beings to pet him on the back, give him his jollies."

"You got some imagination, kid."

"That's why I'm walking guard duty. I'm so bright, they don't know what to do with me, right?"

"R-i-i-i-ght."

By this time, Mark had scampered quietly down the side of the barge and following a hunch, slipped through the doorway of the barge house.

This barge house extended below the waterline, and Mark trotted down a set of stairs to reach its main level. There he found exactly what he was after.

Sunk partway below the narrow entryway were two cells. The lower half of each cell was under water; the upper halves contained cots, sinks, and shelves so that the cells seemed as an ordinary jail flooded to a depth of about four feet.

In the first cell he saw Lioa, asleep under the water. He reached between the bars and rippled the surface. She awakened with a start. Mark put a finger to his lips. While she was orienting herself, Mark looked into the adjoining cell. Xos lay asleep under the water.

Lioa surfaced and came to the bars wearing a silent smile. She nuzzled against the bars, looking at Mark.

He reached in and touched her face. She reached out and touched his.

"Lioa." His voice was soft and soothing.

"Mark."

"I need to speak to you."

"And I to you." She pressed her face to the bars and tried to glimpse into the next cell. "Xos?"

"Asleep."

"Speak softly."

"There is so little time, so much I need to know."

"Yes."

"This symbol was on my clothing, here, when they found me."

She nodded. "The conch in the waves, yes. It is the symbol of our planet."

Mark gripped the bars. "Then we *are* from the same place?" he asked urgently.

"Yes."

"But where? Where is that place we come from, that place about which I have no memory?"

"From the space beyond the nine worlds around your sun."

"It is not my sun."

"No, excuse me. *Their* sun."

"But you speak the same language as the beings here."

"Our voyage was a long sleep. The language was accumulated from space flights, and put into our minds."

"How?"

"Recordings. Played over and over again to our sub-conscious minds. It is a kind of learning better than any other, for your active mind does not resist the strange sounds and syllables."

"But I speak it too."

"You had a long sleep on your voyage, the same as we."

Mark was very tense, and not just because he was worried about the guards. He was tense with the apprehension of one on the threshold of learning who he is. There was a conflict of mind, he longed to know but was afraid of what might be revealed. "I had a voyage?"

"Yes."

"From that same planet? *Our* planet?"

"Yes."

"Why?"

"You were expelled for not believing."

It was a weighty pronouncement. But the question had to be asked. "For not believing what?"

"Later. You cannot understand yet. There is much to which you must be reintroduced. Be patient."

"Patient!" That seemed too much to ask; for who he was and where he came from now mattered more than anything else to him; and he had already been patient for what seemed like forever. "Lioa—you and Xos had to take over other people's bodies to appear as you do."

She backed away a few inches from the bars and averted her eyes. "Yours was done for you, and afterward your mind was blanked."

It hit him in the chest like an ambusher's dart. So he was not even what he seemed to be, not what he had grown accustomed to in mirrors, not what his human friends thought he was. This was not his own body. It was as if, after learning the first few facts about himself, he had less identity than ever. "Then—

what do we look like? What is our original appearance?"

He closed his eyes for the response. But it was mild. "We are small. We are very beautiful."

He opened his eyes to see her smile. "Why did you try to kill me?"

"We were not trying to kill. When we breathe air, we become hostile and afraid. We protect ourselves in the only way we know how."

"But I myself breathe air, and I do not become—"

She put her finger over her lips. "Shhh. Do not expect to learn everything at once, as I told you."

"I meant you no harm."

"We did not know. We could not be sure what you would be like."

Mark studied her face, a face with great beauty by human standards, a lean face, well formed, with deep brown eyes, a full mouth. Why should such a face be attractive to him, whose own world would not contain such a face? Why was Elizabeth Merrill's face so appealing? Was it only because in both these faces there was warmth and friendliness? It was too thorny a subject to pursue. "Why are you so afraid of fire?"

"It is told that on our planet at one time there was much fire that came from the mountains."

"You mean volcanoes?"

"Yes. We breathed air then. But there was fire, and smoke, and ashes, and the people were dying, until they learned to breathe through wetness." To demonstrate, she pulled a towel from the rack above the waterline, soaked it, and held it over her nose. "After much time, children were born able to breathe better through wetness than they could in open air. And finally our race breathed under water. We moved into the sea."

His head ached with this almost total denial of the only mode of living he knew—this betrayal of the body which he thought was his; this assertion that he was nothing familiar at all. Why wasn't *he* afraid of fire?

But no, he would heed her advice not to probe too deeply all at once. "You are afraid of children."

She raised her eyebrows.

"Back there, in the town, two little children frightened you, just by approaching you."

Then she answered, matter-of-factly, "You do not remember. In our world children are the enemy."

He blinked. "That is hard to understand."

"At one time parents were firm and clear in what they believed. But they became weary and unsure of themselves; they no longer understood good or evil, right or wrong, work or idleness, purpose or void. And the children began to hate them. And then to kill them."

"No!"

"It is true."

"Then the world we come from is bad!"

She did not demur, but sat back and looked off through the bars. "We came here to see if this world is a better one."

"Is it?" He pressed closer to the bars, begging for her answer.

"It is. We will signal our leaders to start the invasion."

"Invasion?"

"Yes. We will come and live in the sea. We will organize it for you. You will be the one to mediate between the water people and those on land. You will be as a king."

"No. I am not a king."

"Yes." She reached through the bars and touched his arm. "It was planned that way." She smiled demurely. "Your face, your strength, your kindness—there is a reason for such an appearance. Touch me."

As if in a daze, he reached in to her, putting his fingers on her cheek.

She smiled. "Your touch is the touch of beauty."

Mark was overwhelmed, inundated by the swirl of revelations and emotions. Suddenly his body—a shallow substitute, he knew now, for what he really was—was once again a thing of beauty, the very touch of fingers that didn't belong to him something wonderful.

She looked at him fondly. His gaze was uncertain, proud, vain, reassured, and confused—a volatile mix.

Suddenly her look grew strange, detached. She slumped down into the water.

"Lioa! What is it?"

She pulled herself up to the bars. "I am weak. I need nourishment."

"I will go outside, and dive to the bottom—"

"No. Not that. I need my own special kind of nourishment. Neither that of humans nor that of fish."

"What, then?"

"In the tank in your laboratory, by the small computer. My nourishment is there."

"That plant-stone? The thing that a child brought in?"

"It is what we eat. We can survive for a time with kelp. But the foundation of our nourishment is that. I have been without it for a long time. Do you think you could—"

"Of course!"

He saw her sink further toward the floor. Fearing for her life, he tore up the stairs, paused only to make sure the guards were still occupied, and dove off the barge, so skillfully that he didn't make a splash.

The removal of Xos and Lioa from F.O.R.'s control left many mysteries about them unsolved, of course, and Elizabeth was unable to put them out of her mind. There was other work to which she could have turned, but it paled beside the wonders of that exotic couple.

Though she couldn't deal with them directly any longer, Still she grasped at anything left behind that related to them and their mysteries. She had re-examined the hairs many times; had studied over and over again the various samples and readouts taken from them. There were no new discoveries in this repetition, but it made her feel as if she were still in contact with the couple, however slightly.

Both she and Miller had somehow forgotten the rock-carrot. When she happened to remember it, she was both surprised that she could have forgotten it and elated that it was still there for her examination.

She fairly sprang to the tank. Seeing that it had reverted to its stone shape—when she had last noticed it, it resembled the gray carrot—she was awed and excited.

She did not call Miller immediately. It was quite late at night, and he was probably asleep. And besides, she wanted this precious evidence to herself for a while.

She lifted the stone from the tank and took a scraping with a small knife. When she put the scraping under the microscope, she saw what she and Miller had seen before. The stone was composed of cells, oddly elongated but alive like a plant, not dead like a stone. The nuclei were in motion. Over a period of time a nucleus would move from the center of the cell to the cell wall, then around within it, as if looking for an exit. The nuclei had a purple tint, as if they had been stained for microscopic study. The cell walls had a queer rigidity to them.

Half-plant, half-stone: she named it a "plone," and smiled at her cleverness.

The secret she was after, of course, was what caused it to change from plant to stone and back. Perhaps, she thought, those purplish nuclei were sometimes unable to escape through the cell walls, causing the plant to harden like a rock. She wished she had been smart enough to take a sample from the plant form. They had been so busy with other matters. . . .

But she would watch it and study it and play with it until it changed shape again.

She was still engaged in her study of the strange cells when Mark came silently through the rear door of the lab. For several moments, he stood watching her without speaking and sensing herself under scruteny, her shoulders tensed. She turned slowly to face him. "Mark! I can't believe it!"

He quickly put his finger to his lips.

"I have spoken to Lioa," he said softly.

"What?" She wanted to welcome him gloriously, celebrate his unexpected return. But he was clearly not in the mood. "How could you—"

He held up a palm to stop her. "I learned everything, Elizabeth."

"Everything?" she said breathlessly. "You must tell me! Who are they? Why are they here?"

"First I must take food to her." He quickly went to the tank containing the "plone" and lifted it out, holding it carefully in his hands.

"Mark, must you take that? That's our only physical connection with their world. Couldn't you take her some fresh kelp?"

"They need this. This is their basic nourishment. They will be sick without it. Already Lioa is showing signs of dangerous weakness." He looked around. "Where is the case?"

"The case?"

"Ah." He spotted the tin the boy had brought it in under some papers in the wastebasket. He took it out and put the plone in it. "Do not try to stop me."

"Mark." She rose slowly and stood in front of him, studying his green eyes. "You're different."

"No—"

"Something has changed you."

He hesitated, then put the tin down on the desk and raised his hands to take Elizabeth's shoulders. He spoke tenderly: "I need you and I care for you, Elizabeth. I am not different. But I must do this thing my way."

Elizabeth relaxed slightly, relieved by his words and the tone of his voice. She nodded.

"Call Mr. Stockwood," he continued, "and explain that I am taking food to them. Tell him to have a guard meet me at the main entrance and escort me in."

"Main entrance to what?"

"He will know. Do not ask me to tell you everything now. I have little time. She is very weak." He looked into her eyes. "Elizabeth, trust me."

"Yes." The request magically restored, for her, the strong bond between them. "Yes, I will. I'll call him right now."

"Thank you.

They looked at each other for a few silent seconds, then he picked up the tin and backed toward the door.

By the time he reached it, Elizabeth was already dialing.

It was as he had requested. Two guards met him at the main shore gate, escorted him in the skiff out to the barge. The two barge guards helped him aboard, opened the barge-house door, and allowed him to pass down to the cells.

The guards remained outside, watching through the open door. Moonlight spilled down the stairs and a shaft of it filled Lioa's cell.

He went quickly to the bars and held up the tin. Slumped under the water, Lioa nodded weakly. He tried to push the tin between the bars, but it was too large. He took out the plone, stuck it through, and dropped it into the water.

Lioa pulled herself over to it as it sank. Mark stared at her with urgent concern. She smiled wanly, holding the plone against her chest. "You are—" she seemed to be searching for a word "—wondrous?" She nodded, satisfied with her choice. "Because of you, we will eat well. And sleep well. I hope they will let you come again tomorrow."

"I cannot bring you more of those plant-rocks. That is the only one they had."

"It is sufficient. No, I did not mean that you must bring more nourishment, only that I hope you can come and talk to me."

He gazed at her rapturously.

She stared out along the shaft of light. "We do not have such a moon," she said softly. "Or trees. Or hills covered with green and clouded over with white, or such sweet smells."

"This world is pleasing to you."

"Yes."

"It can be yours, as it is mine."

"It will be ours."

Mark took a deep and luxurious breath.

She reached out and and touched his cheek. "Good night."

"Good night."

Mark turned and looked up at the guard, who impatiently shifted his weight from foot to foot. He glanced a final time at Lioa, returned her smile, and went up the stairs.

The guard closed the door behind Mark and escorted him back to the waiting skiff.

Elizabeth tossed uncomfortably in her bed. She herself was not sure whether she was asleep or awake. Nightmares or dark thoughts; dreams or ominous musings; whichever they were, they caused her to worm and thrash under the sheets.

When at last she opened her eyes to see the moonlit room, and the moon itself hovering in splendid isolation in the ether, thoughts or dreams stayed with her, as clear as they had been seconds or minutes or hours before.

She tried to sort and focus them, set them arow, force them into a manageable pattern; she wanted them in proper order for analysis, so she could derive some concusion from the jumble.

How much of this, she thought, can a single human mind handle before there is an overload? How expandable is the scientific brain, how many facts and emotions can it house simultaneously? Is it, as some say, limitless, with an infinity of storage space which can never be filled? Or is it, as others believe, a finite clump of nodules and passageways and neurons which, when capacity is reached, shuts down?

But there was, after all, a pattern emerging, though faint. There was, as Stockwood said, a likelihood. Her face clouded over. It was not a scientific conclusion she reached, but an altogether human one, a feeling, a sense that caused her alarm.

Suddenly she swung her legs off the bed, shed her nightgown, pulled on her skirt and white smock, and headed for the stairs.

Her feeling was redoubled when, as she entered the lab, Mark stepped in through the back door.

"Mark! Yes, it's perfect timing! I have to talk to you. I have figured something out!"

"Yes! And now I want to tell you all that I have learned!"

chapter 9

Xos was erect in his cell, leaning against the wall which divided it from Lioa's, listening intently to the soft sounds. "Does it function?" he whispered.

There was no immediate answer.

Lioa was in the rear of her cell, on her knees, holding the plone—still in its stone form—on the floor and kneading it with her hands. Repeatedly she pressed down on it, lifted her hands, pressed down again, almost as if she were given it artificial respiration. As she labored over the plone, gritting her teeth, the muscles of her arms were taut.

"Lioa, does it function?" came the insistent whisper.

She picked up the plone and examined it, turning it over in her hands. She pursed her lips and shook her head. "I am trying," she whispered back.

She returned to her task, pressing and releasing, pressing and releasing.

"Quickly! They said they were going to bring in a recovery vessel! They will raise our craft!"

Lioa increased the speed of her ministrations to the plone. At last it gradually started to alter its shape and texture. Faster she pressed and released. The plone was no longer a rock. It was flexible. She kneaded it more.

At last it took on its other form: the tapered shape of a common carrot, gray, with a smooth exterior. She stopped her actions and held it up and looked at it with a smile of relief. "Xos! It functions now! It is ready!"

"Good! Are you also prepared?"

"I am!"

"Then we shall proceed at once! I am again as if asleep."

Lioa felt the surface of the plone and re-examined every inch of it. She took a deep breath. Then, holding the plone, she moved to the front of the cell and began to moan. She moaned louder. After a few moans the door above the stairs opened and a guard looked in.

"Something the matter down there?"

She moaned more. He came cautiously down the stairs and stood a few feet from her cell.

"What's the trouble?"

"Ooooh," she moaned, looking up at him plaintively.

He stepped to the bars. "Are you sick?"

She nodded.

He squatted down to bring his face close to hers. "Can you tell me exactly what—"

Suddenly she thrust the plone between the bars and squeezed it. Its tiny tip emitted a cloud of purple fog.

As the cloud enveloped the guard, he reacted as if stung all over. He dropped to his knees and fell against the bars, covering his face with his hands, writhing. After a brief, lively moment, he lost consciousness.

Lioa reached out and grabbed his belt and pulled his body close. She patted the material around his pockets until she found the lump of keys. She pulled them out, worked them up to the outside of the lock, and opened her cell.

She slipped out and went next door. Xos was gripping the bars eagerly as she turned the key in his lock.

They crouched their way to the stairs and scurried up them, Xos a step behind Lioa. She opened the door a crack, and heard the footsteps of the second guard approaching.

"Sam?" he called.

When he was at the door, she suddenly swung it open and squirted the purple fluid at him.

Like the first, this guard fell prostrate on the deck.

They moved quickly to the rail. Glancing back, Xos saw one of the guard's legs move slightly. "We must kill them!"

"There's no need," Lioa said, tugging at his hand.

Together they dropped into the water and disappeared under it.

Mark and Elizabeth were sitting facing each other across her desk. She sipped from a cup of coffee. Mark had recounted carefully and thoroughly his meetings with Lioa, though treading lightly on the matter of "invasion," calling it instead a "larger visitation," and suggesting that, with his help, such an event would be tempered; surely he could convince them to abandon that scheme to stay in peace, and be a friend like him.

She had listened patiently, not interrupting, keeping her eyes on him, sensing the enormous importance of what he was telling her.

"So," he said after a pause, "it is true that I am one of them."

She poured another cup of coffee. "Mark, there's

something that I want to say." Feeling his eyes on her, she looked down at her cup and picked her words deliberately. "A strange thought woke me just before you got here."

"Tell me of your thought."

"Well, after everything you've told me, and how you feel about it, and what you've been through, you're not going to like this. But Mark," she leaned across the desk on her elbows, "I think she was lying to you."

"No." He shook his head rapidly.

"Remember the moment Xos started to talk?" she resumed quickly, wanting to transmit her message to him before he had a chance to resist. "He became aware that Stockwood would go after his spacecraft. He stalled that by saying he'd cooperate. Mark, they know *exactly* what they're doing. They're so advanced, we can't even keep up with them."

"It is not wrong that they know what they are doing," he said firmly, "just as we know what we are doing."

"But what I mean is, it's a ploy, a stall for time. I'm sure of it. There are so many small things that came together for me all at once. Why, after being so resistant and hostile, would they suddenly become entirely cooperative? To buy time, Mark, to formulate a plan."

"No. If you had heard her, and seen her talking to me, you wouldn't say that. Perhaps in my telling of it I was not as convincing as she. What she told me was complete and logical. And it was true."

"Mark," she said. She reached to touch his hand, but he withdrew it. "Your yearning to know the truth about yourself is natural and understandable. I ache along with you in your search. But it's become an obsession with you, and it's clouding your mind. It's eroding your usual brilliance and perception. . . ."

"Why won't you believe me?" His voice was like a mournful call.

She felt he needed to hear stronger words. "All right. I won't believe you because I think you're afraid to admit that you've been tricked into falling in love."

He snapped up straight, staring at her.

"That's right. We're all afraid to look at that kind of pain—the kind of pain that warps your thinking and your feelings. You *know* deep down inside that what you heard from her has to be a lie!"

"No—"

"You're *not* like them! You're *not* afraid of fire! You're *not* afraid of children! You *feel*. You're like *us*! Face it, Mark! Look at it! Use that great strength and determination you have to see what the truth really is!"

She let it sink in. It did so visibly. Mark shook his head slowly. He opened his mouth and closed it. He rubbed his eyes with the back of his hand. He got up and paced beside the desk, looking at the floor, then the ceiling.

The telephone rang. She picked it up, still watching Mark. "F.O.R. Dr. Merrill. What?" She rose quickly from her chair. "When? Oh no! I understand. Thank you." She held the receiver in front of her and looked at it as she slowly put it down. From it came faint sounds of alarm bells and sirens.

"Mark, they've escaped," she said softly, though her words stopped him cold. "The purple fluid was used on the guards. The place is in a panic, naturally. The

Navy wants them, and their spacecraft. And Mark?"
They locked eyes. "You have to help."

Mark sank back into his chair. For a few moments
he was silent, shaking his head off and on. He looked
at her with eyes grown weary and sad—a look she had
not seen from him before. "How do I know what the
Navy told you is true?" he asked in a bitter tone.
"How do I know they weren't forced into doing what
they are said to have done?"

Elizabeth stood before him as if at attention. Her
face was firm. "Mark, I have to go get ready. There is
a most difficult time ahead of us. With you or without
you, Miller and I have to go." She paused. "Will you
help us?"

He rose slowly from his chair, his splendid, muscu-
lar body seeming to creak like that of an old man. He
went to the picture window and looked out at the
moon-bathed sea.

She remained standing as she was, looking not at
him but at where he had been, at his chair, just as if
he still sat there.

He turned and looked at her averted face, at the
lovely profile of his initial savior and constant friend.

"What do you say?" she snapped. For her, all had
been said. She could add nothing to what she had just
said, or over the many months they had been together. To summon all her own strength for what lay
ahead, she now demanded a simple yes or no. For all
her emotional ties, she was not so frail and vulnerable
a woman. She would go on with it, either way.

Faint shivers roamed through Mark's body, rippling
along his legs and arms and across his chest. He
looked down at his hands—possibly owned, possibly
borrowed—and slowly brought them up in front of his

face. He spread his fingers and stared at the webbing between them.

Activity in the sub pen was professionally frantic. Wes and his crew raced about in the sub and outside it, stowing gear and double-checking systems. Wes seldom barked a command, so well drilled was the carefully chosen crew. For all the hurrying, there were no collisions, no missteps, no motions wasted.

The only exception to the latter was with C.W. Crawford, whose prancing back and forth, jumping out of the way of hustling crewmen and immediately stumbling back into it, waggling his arms like a jacketed scarecrow in a breeze, was the very epitome and definition of motion wasted, albeit harmlessly.

Elizabeth and Miller strode briskly from the tunnel toward the sub, then stood aside while final preparations were made by the crew.

After a moment, Mark came slowly from the tunnel. He did not cross the pier, but stood back by the wall, watching silently.

They did not see him.

"Did he say anything? Miller asked.

"No. I don't know if he's going to help us or not."

"What do you suspect?"

"I don't. It's out of my hands."

Miller watched the crew pensively. "It's hard enough when you're born here. Go try to explain this life to someone from an unknown place." He shook his head. "What an unfathomably difficult spot for him. I don't blame him, do you?"

"No. He just can't accept it, what I told him."

With a tentative step, Mark had moved over behind them. "I accept it."

They whirled to confront him.

"I can face the truth."

They did not smile or clap him on the back.

"Okay," Miller said sternly, "what is the truth?"

"I—" He seemed puzzled and unsure.

"The truth is," Elizabeth said coolly, "you're in love with her."

Mark examined her face with humble, searching eyes. "How is that possible if she's dangerous and harmful?"

Recognizing Mark's plight and his painful vulnerability, Elizabeth softened her gaze, and Miller softened his words.

"It happens all the time," Miller said. "When you love someone it doesn't make any difference if they're dangerous or not."

"I do not understand loving then."

"Join the crowd."

"We don't either, Mark," Elizabeth said soothingly. "It gets very mixed up with the feelings that can come from touching and smelling and seeing and needing and hoping. It has very little to do with reasoning."

"But you asked me to reason."

"There is a time when that is necessary to sort out the mixture of feelings."

Crawford came stomping over. "I mean, this is crazy with you three. We're stalling national defense—international defense! What are you guys talking about, birds and bees?"

"C.W.?" Elizabeth said sweetly.

"Yes?"

"Shut up! You're such a boob sometimes."

"Hunh? Ump. Erp." He backed away a few steps. "You don't think I'm bad for what I have done?"

Mark went on. "You don't think I'm sick, or crazy, for feeling what I feel about someone who may be evil?"

"Oh Mark," she touched his cheek, "you're not bad. You say it like such a child, as if you've been whipped and might be sent to bed without any supper. No, Mark, don't feel crushed by what we have told you. You aren't at all diminished in our eyes." She chuckled. "You may be a little sick, just now. But you'll get over it. We all do."

The captain waited atop the conning tower. Crawford glanced up at him, then took a step toward the three. "You're responsible for trying to stop those foreigners from sending for millions more just like them, don't forget!"

"Aye-aye, C.W.," Elizabeth said, saluting him smartly. "Mark?"

He stared into her eyes. "I'm over it," he said firmly.

"Then let's go."

They waved to Wes, who nodded back. Then they hurried across the gangplank. Wes stepped out of the conning-tower hatch to let them pass. "Cast off!" he shouted to the dock crew. Then he followed the others down into the sub.

Wes went through launching procedures and check-offs. "The con is closed. The con is locked. What'll it be, Dr. Merrill?"

"We're going directly to the spacecraft."

"Roger. That's familiar enough territory." He leaned closer to the intercom. "Take her down! Ten meters!"

The Klaxon blasted. Water rushed into the ballast tanks. The smooth hum of the engines rose as the turbines delivered first power. The sub settled down just under the surface.

"Reverse slow!"

The throb of the propellers vibrated through the hull. The sub began backing slowly out of the pen.

Wes watched the monitors to see when the sub had cleared its confines. "All stop!" He waited for the thrust to subside. "Ahead slow! Half right rudder!"

The sub drifted for a few seconds, then eased forward, turning neatly to face the sea.

Lights burned into the ocean ahead of them and lit the surrounding water from the ports. On more pleasurable and less dramatic trips, Elizabeth and Miller liked to look out the ports, shunning the electronic monitors to watch directly with their own eyes the shimmering colors, the curious schools of darting fish, the wriggling squid or occasional porpoise or nosy grouper that followed them. It was an enchanting world, a dreamy reality full of mystery and promise and treasures to discover.

And peril. The portholes held no interest for them now. They stood tensely near the speakers and monitors and readouts, fearfully anticipating sights and events toward which they glided steadily.

Wes had toured the ship to inspect all stations, and now returned to their sphere. "The Navy has put four choppers in the air with frogmen."

"What are frogmen supposed to do?" Elizabeth asked irritably.

Wes shrugged. "Who knows? Precautionary, probably."

"Jim, anything on the scope yet?"

"No, ma'am," replied the second officer, hunched closely over his sonar scope. "Not yet. But the Navy is trying to track them from the air. Bobby-K is monitoring that."

"As if you could pick them up from a plane like whales," Miller mused.

The four huge Navy Sikorskys twenty meters above the surface of the sea were two hundred meters away from each other. The helmeted pilots peered down into the water. At the large open side doors, tethered frogmen also scanned the view.

One pilot spoke. "This is Two-oh-one. You guys see anything down there?"

"This is Two-four-four," came the reply over the radio. "Negative, Two-oh-one."

"Three-six-one," came another voice, "also negative."

For a minute the choppers thumped ahead, like giant grasshoppers wearing rotor-topped beanies. Seen from the water or from another helicopter, their flight appeared smooth, but it was not. The choppers bounced and swung in the currents of warm air which rose from the ocean. Flying at this low altitude, in the turbulence always generated from the sea, required the constant attention of the pilots. They maneuvered their levers and foot pedals incessantly, correcting for the jouncing and swirling air that tended to disturb their course and altitude.

The frogmen at their jump stations, seasoned veterans trained as paramedics as well as in combat, stood and swayed in apparent casualness. But they were not casual. They did not converse. Their thoughts were on their checklists; their eyes were on the water flashing by below.

"This is Two-oh-one," came the pilot's voice abruptly. "I see something." His co-pilot was nodding at his side, his eyes trained on the same spot. "It's faint, but it might be something. Why don't you guys come over here and join us for a look?"

The four choppers veered in their pattern to the north.

"That's it! That's it!" It was the voice of the chief frogman in chopper 201. "There they are! Take us down and drop us!"

The lead chopper slowed and dropped, finally hovering a few feet above the swells. Quickly four frogmen leaped from the doors and splashed into the water, disappearing amid the plumes of spray sent up by their entry.

The near-silence of the sub, unaffected by the swells or the wind, gliding smoothly along the womb of the sea, had a hypnotic effect on the scientists and crew.

Whatever reveries they entertained were broken harshly by the voice of Bobby-K. "We have the Navy on monitor."

"Let's hear it," Elizabeth said into the mike.

There was a momentary delay while Bobby-K punched it up.

Then the speakers rasped: "Two-oh-one to Base! Two-oh-one to Base!"

A pause. "Go ahead, Two-oh-one."

"We've just lost four frogmen! We spotted those strangers and dropped our frogmen, and two minutes later they surfaced. They seemed to be gasping for air! They had torn off their regulators and were clawing at their throats! There's some purple chemical spreading over the water in the area! Asking permission to call for depth bombs!"

Miller grabbed the mike. "Bobby-K! Give me Navy frequency for sending!"

Mark brushed by Elizabeth. "I must go now." He raced for the main airlock, Elizabeth at his heels.

"Go ahead and on Navy frequency," Bobby-K said.

"Foxtrot Oscar Roger to Two-oh-one!" Miller hugged the mike.

"Two-oh-one. Go ahead, Foxtrot Oscar Roger."

"Hold everything! Don't call for bombs! We have a man in the water, and we don't have his position!"

Miller waited an eternity for the answer that came in seconds.

"Two-oh-one to Foxtrot Oscar Roger. Let us know as soon as he is clear. Two-oh-one out."

Miller leaned back and let his breath escape between clenched teeth in a long, low whistle. Then he jumped up and headed for the airlock.

Mark stood by the open door. The airlock man was poised at his station.

"Are you all right, Mark?" Elizabeth asked.

"Yes. I told you, I am over it."

"They've got that chemical."

"I need flares."

"Wes! Flares, on the double!"

"Roger," he said on the intercom. "Coming right up."

"What should *we* do, Mark?" Miller asked.

"Stay. Wait."

Wes arrived with a fistful of flares. Mark took two of them, stuffed them into his waistband, and stepped into the lock.

Elizabeth nodded to the airlock man, and he swung the heavy door shut, sealed it, and pulled the levers that caused water to flood in and replace the air.

Mark emerged from the airlock, limbered his muscles briskly, and undulated away from the sub. Knowing that Elizabeth and Miller would be watching him on the minitors, and that he would soon be out of range, he turned once and waved good-bye to his unseen associates.

Then, at high speed, he headed away and down into the trench. He no longer needed to chart his course by visual signs and markings along the canyon; the path was etched in his memory and instincts like scrollwork on the hilt of a blade.

He sensed, but didn't see or look for, the presence of Xos and Lioa in the water. The vibrations could be coming from far away, from any direction. He slid through the water like an undulating spear; he went faster and faster, like a runner mustering his strength for the last stretch.

Then the spacecraft's entry tube glimmered like a diamond in the distance, grew and took shape as he zoomed toward it.

When he reached it, he did not perform his usual inspection tour around its rim, but dove into it straightway, plunging down to alight on the spacecraft's floor.

A quick look around assured him that he was the first to arrive. But something new caught his eye. A strange plaque, or rather half a plaque, hung on the wall, with flowing symbols cut off abruptly at the broken edges.

Had it been there before? He couldn't be sure. But

he doubted it. Yet as surely as he didn't remember it, it reminded him of something.

He stooped to the floor and picked up the shard he had found before, with the conch-and-waves design that matched the symbol on his trunks. He brought it up and put it beside the plaque hanging on the wall. Slowly he moved them together, the broken edges fitting precisely. As one, they formed a perfect triangle, point down, showing now two curlicued eyes—like conches—and one long arcing mouth—like waves.

He stepped back and stared intently at the picture. It was a face, a small one, odd but delicate, and beautiful in a haunting way. A gentle visage, though strained with tears and agony.

The vibrations were closer. He cocked his head and listened, or felt.

Abruptly he darted up through the tunnel and out.

He raced for an outcropping of rock and slid behind it just as Xos and Lioa came into his view.

They moved past him toward the tube, seemingly oblivious to his presence.

But surely they sensed his vibrations in the water, as he had theirs.

He swam quickly after them, and then called sharply, "Lioa!"

Lioa, to the rear of Xos, turned to see him. Xos continued ahead.

Was it possible that they hadn't sensed him? Weren't they just like him? He beckoned to Lioa.

She stopped, and looked one way toward the retreating Xos, then the other way toward the advancing Mark. She seemed uncertain. She waited for him. In one hand she held the plone.

Then Xos, near the tube, stopped and slowly turned

around. His eyes flashed angrily. He motioned to the plone, and held up his hand as if to squeeze it.

She looked at the plone, then back and forth between them. She brought the plone up, but didn't point it at Mark, or squeeze it.

Xos gestured more vigorously, beginning to move back in her direction. Repeatedly he pointed his arm and squeezed his fist, scowling at her.

She lowered the plone and slowly shook her head.

Responding as if that were his signal, Mark closed on her, took her hand, and pulled her away from the approaching Xos.

His mouth in a snarl, his eyes narrowed to slits, Xos was enraged. He hurled himself through the water to reach Lioa, and shoved her into Mark while he wrested the plone from her hand.

Mark pushed Lioa to the side and hovered, waiting for Xos to aim. He darted from side to side as Xos moved in on him. Suddenly Lioa lunged between them, shielding Mark from the plone. As Xos moved to one side, she grabbed his arm and yanked it down.

Xos swung his other arm viciously at her, smacking her across the head and sending her tumbling away. Xos, his face contorted cruelly, dove after her, aimed the plone at her, and squeezed.

The poison shot into the water, enveloping her instantly. She stiffened and cried out silently.

In the aftermath of his impulsive act, Xos hovered, staring at her.

She grimaced and put a hand to her side. Her body twitched convulsively. She turned and began swimming unevenly toward the tube. The flexibility of her body diminished; she could no longer undulate smoothly but had to crab along in an awkward side-stroke.

She dropped into the tube like a stone.

Mark tried to follow her, but Xos quickly interposed himself, pointing the plone at him.

Mark eluded him; for all their similarities Xos was no match for Mark as a swimmer. He darted low and slipped around behind the tube, keeping it between himself and Xos.

Lioa hauled herself over to the wall of the chamber with the two red buttons showing two halves of a spewing volcano—separated by a spreader bar. Painfully she reached up to seize the bar. It didn't yield to her hand. She grabbed it with both hands and yanked downward. It slipped a bit from its notches. On the next try it gave. She pulled it free and tucked it behind a loose angular surface on the wall.

Then even more painfully she hoisted herself up along the wall to reach the two buttons. With a great consolidation of her waning strength, she shoved the two together, completing the picture of the volcano.

Immediately throughout the craft there echoed the insistent whines of an alarm siren. The lighting system flashed on and off.

She backed away from the wall, her face awash in sadness and pain.

Then, with laborious strokes of her arms, she pulled herself back into the tunnel and tried to go up.

The wailing of the alarms spread through the surrounding ocean, causing Xos to look toward the tube with eyes wide in panic. Holding the plone in front of him to force Mark back from the entrance, Xos swam to the tube. Waving the plone one last threatening time, he dove inside.

After hesitating a moment, Mark dove in behind him.

Lioa had not been able to make the ascent through the tube. She had fallen back, and now lay crumpled in a corner of the faceted chamber.

Xos went immediately to the two buttons. Using one hand, he tried to pull the buttons apart. They held fast. He dropped the plone and attacked with both hands, straining against their weld.

The plone fell to the floor and drifted to a corner near the control panel, accompanied in its graceful tumbling by the continuing raw howl of the alarms and the rhythmic flashing of the lights.

Mark slipped from the tube and went immediately to Lioa's side, unnoticed by Xos who was occupied with the buttons.

Xos left the buttons and began frantically searching for the spreader bar that Lioa had hidden. Unable to find it immediately, he returned to his ferocious clawing at the locked buttons.

Lioa's voice was faint and trembling. "Our ship . . . is going to . . . explode. You must . . . flee . . ."

"With you! I will take you with me!"

She closed her eyes and groaned.

At the sound, Xos spun around to them. He dove for Lioa and grabbed her savagely by the neck. "The bar!" he screamed. "Tell me where is the bar!"

Mark tried to push him off, beating at him with hands and fists. But Xos held her in a death-grip.

He remembered the flares. He pulled one from his waistband and yanked the ignition strip. The flame shot out toward Xos. Instantly he dropped Lioa and fell back, holding his hands in front of his face.

Mark heaved Lioa up under his arm and backed toward the entry tube, keeping the flare pointed at Xos.

But once there was some distance between himself and the flare, Xos sprang back to the buttons. Now a red light, shaped like a flame, moved down the wall toward the buttons, lowering toward the cone of the etched volcano. The buttons began to pulse, their red glow dancing on the grotesquely cruel and terrified face of the struggling Xos.

"No . . . time . . ." Lioa gasped. "Go . . . now. It does not matter . . . with me . . ."

Mark dropped the flare. He put one foot on either side of Lioa's neck and clamped her tight. Then, his undulations thus limited, and using his arms in a breaststroke, he began to work his way up the tube, Lioa dangling limp beneath him.

The flare hit the floor, and then rolled and drifted toward the corner where the plone lay.

Xos' howl merged with that of the alarm as he saw the flamelike light descend the wall, now just a few inches above the pulsing buttons. His fingers were raw, his hands cramped. He beat on the buttons with his fists.

In a sudden flash of mental clarity brought on by his desperation, Xos knew where the spreader bar was. He sprang aside to the angular surface behind which there was a narrow space—produced, due to a minor defect in workmanship that seemed unimportant at the time, when the ship wrenched through the earth's atmosphere.

In there he saw the bar. He could not uncoil his ravaged fingers. He slammed a fist into the crevasse, loosening the surface more, and hooked his hand around the bar and pulled it out in the crook of his wrist.

He forced the bar under his curled fingers and jabbed its pointed end at the spot where the buttons met. A slight separation appeared between them.

But in the far corner of the room, under the control panel, the fiery flare had come to rest against the plone. The flame hissed against its skin. And suddenly, like a wounded animal lashing out against an attacker, the plone erupted, spewing a thick cloud of purple poison into the chamber.

Xos was near success in prying the buttons apart when the fog swept over him. He gasped, clutched his throat, staggered backward, and fell, still clutching the spreader bar.

The buttons instantly slid back together. The flame-light in the wall sunk to the top of the volcano.

Mark pulled Lioa from the tube opening and away toward the outcropping where he had hidden earlier. Once separated from the half-buried spacecraft, he lay her out along the protected side. He stroked her hair, her forehead, her back, her arms. Her breath grew shorter and shorter.

And so he knew he had to move on. He slung her over his back, hooking her arms around his neck, and began digging his way through the dark Pacific in the direction of the waiting submersible.

Then an explosion rent the ocean floor around the spacecraft, boiled the sea, and hurled Mark and Lioa head over heels against a rock ledge.

Aftershocks slammed them into the rocks again and again.

At last it was still. Mark shook his head to clear the grogginess and stared dazedly around, trying to get his bearings. He was some distance from the ship, not within sonar range. But if Bobby-K was good enough . . .

"We're here!" he shouted into the sea. "Come to my voice! There is no further danger! But she is hurt! You must hurry!"

Bobby-K was good enough: the voice coming over his unique system triggered the crew into action.

"Left rudder!" Wes bellowed. "Ahead full!"

The sub angled to port and picked up speed quickly. They had been lying near enough to the spacecraft to feel the sub heave as if it were under attack from depth charges. In minutes they were near enough to see, on the monitors, Mark with Lioa cradled in his arms, huddled under the ledge of rock.

Mark left the ledge and rose toward the ship.

"Mark and injured female approaching main airlock!" Wes sang out.

Elizabeth and Miller and several of the crew gathered anxiously around the lock.

They came quickly through. Mark, still groggy, dazed, and weak from the effects of the explosions, let four crewmen lift the unconscious Lioa from his arms and rush her aft to the sick-bay operating table.

Staggering slightly, Mark followed Elizabeth and Miller to the stern sphere.

Lioa was stretched out on the table, and Elizabeth examined her quickly with hands and stethoscope.

Aides wheeled over a tray of medical equipment, but Elizabeth waved them off.

"You must save her!" Mark cried.

Lioa opened her eyes slightly and looked at him. "I want to live," she said in a faint voice, "in the air . . . like you . . ."

"You must save her! With your tools! You are a doctor, Elizabeth!"

Elizabeth bent over Lioa, her voice calm. "Lioa, our equipment on board this sub is not what I need. It will not work for you. But I've already radioed ahead for special equipment, what I need to help you live. It will be waiting at the dock when we arrive. Meanwhile we will do everything we possibly can to make you comfortable. You must be strong and brave."

"Yes," came her piteously weak reply. Her head lolled toward Mark. "I want to be well . . . to know you more."

He took her hand and pressed it between both of his. "Rest, rest," he said gently. "Keep your thoughts on becoming well."

"I think . . . I am the only one . . . in the history of the universe . . ." Her voice trailed off.

"The only one what?" He bent close to her.

"To come from one planet . . . to try to feel so much . . . for someone . . . from another . . ." A spasm stiffened and stifled her. Then she calmed. "I would like to live . . . but I don't think . . . I can."

"You will, Lioa!"

"Not in this body . . . it is not mine."

"Maybe that will change—"

"When you were in the spacecraft—"

"Hush, Lioa, save your strength."

"This I must say. Did you see . . . hanging on the wall—"

"The triangle with the curled eyes?"

"Yes. That was . . . an image of me."

"You are beautiful."

She smiled, but it was a smile limned with pain. It lightened her face but briefly, before she died.

A pleasant, warm sun beat down on the pleasant, calm Pacific. Mark and Elizabeth walked slowly along the bluff.

"I know how you must feel," she said. "My heart aches for you."

"No, Elizabeth," he said soberly, "you must learn not to let my problems affect you so. You have your own problems. We must not let our problems intrude upon each other's peace. There's too much to do, too much to learn."

"That's true," she said, concealing a smile.

"I think you carry too much weight on your shoulders." He turned to her. "Perhaps you need a vacation."

"Yes, perhaps. Not just now. I'm anxious to return to my work."

"We must never let what happened on Lioa's planet happen here," he went on musingly. "So many things have to be guarded, protected, cared for. The fish in the sea. The plants and animals on the land. Even the people. Yes, especially the people. That's something I must learn more about. I must learn, for example, how to know when someone is telling the truth, and when not. . . ."

They walked a while in silence, the wind ruffling their hair. She felt so proud of him, so hopeful. The splendid panorama of the ocean was once again an emblem of her hopeful view of things.

"And now, Elizabeth." He stopped, took her shoulders, and turned her to him. "I will leave you for a while."

She stiffened.

"I would like to go up on the widow's walk, where you go, to stand for a while, and see what you see. And then I will come back down. I would like to take a nap in the tank. And I do not believe you have completed your salinity tests."

She laughed in relief and delight.

"Sometimes I wonder," Miller said, with a wry smile, "about the depth of your feelings for Mark."

"Don't worry. We're like family." She held up her hands and spread her fingers. Don't you see the webbing?"

"Nope."

"Miller," she pouted, "you have no soul."

"My soul, dear Elizabeth, which was old and shriveled and in disrepair, I sold, to start this blasted foundation!"

They laughed heartily and took each other's hands and swung cheerfully into the lab to go to work.